The Battle of
St. George Without

Books by Janet McNeill

The Battle of
St. George Without

by Janet McNeill

Illustrated by
MARY RUSSON

Little, Brown and Company
BOSTON   TORONTO

LIBRARY OF CONGRESS CATALOG CARD NO. 68–11113

FIRST AMERICAN EDITION

PRINTED IN THE UNITED STATES OF AMERICA

The Battle of
St. George Without

~ I ~

HE didn't want a row over the cat. He hadn't even wanted the cat. It was the cat's idea.

"You know we couldn't!" cried his mother, Mrs. McGinley, making him feel foolish for having imagined that perhaps they could. She looked at the animal whose striped stomach squirmed in Matt's hand while its legs fought indignantly against the air. "You know we couldn't keep it ourselves!" With her dishmop she prodded the cups that were floating about in the washing-up water, so that they jiggled against each other, but she seemed too fussed and bothered to pick them out. "A cat could lead to all kinds of trouble." The way she said it, it could have been a wounded rhinoceros or a smoking volcano or a time bomb.

"It is a very small cat," Matt said, but it sounded as if he was reading a line out of a school reading book.

"Small cats grow."

He held onto the cat while the hopeless feeling tightened inside him. He'd been afraid she would be like this. All the way home and while they were eating their tea he'd been afraid. He watched the beads of water at the ends of the taps swell and lengthen, trying to guess the exact moment when they would turn into silver arrows and fall among the floating cups.

"Where did you find it, Matt?"

"I didn't. It found me."

She sighed. "They always do."

This was true. Anything in the animal or bird line that was in difficulties seemed to have got hold of Matt's address as if he was a Do Good Agency or something. It

wasn't his fault, he didn't invite them, he wasn't even particularly glad to see them. Sometimes he thought they did it out of spite or because they were downright lazy. They fell out of bushes in front of him or lay down where he would trip over them. "We're hungry, Matt," they said, "we're lost. We've got thorns in our paws, or our wings are broken, or there's tar on our feet. Find us a home and clean us and feed us and look after us until we're better." And whenever he could, he did. But finding homes was never easy, and parking places for cats in the neighborhood were growing scarce. Old ladies who used to be sympathetic now saw him coming and ran home and locked their doors. So this time he had taken a chance and the cat had come home with him.

"You shouldn't have allowed it to," his mother said.

He was afraid he would begin to mind about the cat just because she didn't mind. So he began to tell her how he had been coming back from school by the ordinary way, the way he came and went every day, so that the meeting between the cat and himself was something that just happened without either of them having done anything about it.

"And after I'd turned the Post Office corner I went into the Ice Cream Shop and bought one —"

"You bought —"

"It was my own money. And only a threepenny one. And I came through the alley and up the steps and halfway up I sat down to eat it. And it came. It just came."

He wondered if it would help if he told her how cunningly it had come, one minute no hint at all of a cat up the steps or down them, and the next minute this cat, pretending to be a piece of sliding sunshine with the stripes on its coat copying the shadows of the railings, until it halted a couple of feet from him and seemed to hook its eyes into the ice cream that was melting in his hand. And how it had crept paw by paw towards the sticky fingers he held out, taking its time. Even when it was within tongue's reach it hesitated, to make the best of what was coming. He knew why it was doing it, he did the same thing with an ice cream himself. Once the tongue reached him it never missed a stroke. And when his fingers were scraped clean he said, "Shoo! That's all. The rest's mine." But it never budged, just sat there purring louder than was decent and looking at him dotingly.

"Get lost, greedy guts," he said, and rummaged in his pocket for the top of a lemonade bottle and threw it at the cat, who dodged and went on purring. And an old lady coming creaking up the steps with a string bag full of oranges said, "What are you doing to poor puss?" and the cat waited until she'd gone past and then winked at him. And after that the cat walked home behind him, never coming really close but always there when he turned to look, and it had lain soberly and humbly on his bed all the time they were having tea, trusting Matt to choose the best moment to introduce it to his mother.

Mrs. McGinley stared at the cat and the cat stared back, as if they were having a competition to see who could go longest without blinking. The cat won. It opened its mouth and a pink whisper of a miaow escaped. His mother pushed the frizzy bit of hair back from her forehead and held out her hand. Matt watched them, and hoped. But her hand was wet and soapy, and the cat reared away from it and spat.

"It's a young dragon you've got there," Mrs. McGinley said, rubbing her hand on her apron.

6

The dragon wriggled from Matt's grasp and jumped for the open window and sat on the outer sill, tidying its fur and taking no notice of anybody.

"There!" Mrs. McGinley said. "That's that. It can look after itself. Close the window, Matt."

"I can't."

"Why?"

"It's left its tail inside."

So it had. Well, that was cunning. An innocent length of orange fur ringed with black. The cat was occupied with what was going on outside the window and had forgotten that anything at all was joined on at the back. Maybe now his mother would laugh.

"You know we couldn't, Matt," she cried again, as if the cat's joke made her angry. "We have to be careful."

"That's what you always say," he growled.

So she did, ever since the day they'd moved into the city and had come to live in Dove Square. That was two years ago and she was still being careful, careful not to offend the neighbors and to wash out the milk bottles properly, careful never to be the first to speak and not to say very much when she did, careful how she spent the money she earned at Mr. Ricardo's Restaurant and not to mind the evenings she had to work late when it wasn't her turn, careful not to hear when other people gave noisy parties and never to use more than her rightful yards of the washing line that she shared with all the other families who lived on the floors above and below them. Life was an obstacle race that Mrs. McGinley ran against herself, and she never allowed herself to win.

The cat on the second-floor sill was bored with both of them, and Matt, because his face was burning with plain ordinary crossness, went and joined it at the window, looking out. He was cross with himself because he minded. But other people had dogs and cats and budgies — Henry Mickle had had white mice once — and they had rows with their neighbors over them and kept on having dogs and cats and budgies. Why couldn't she be like other people?

The houses in Dove Square were large and solid, most of them four-storied with a basement below and attic windows rising from the roof. Walls were peeling and the blistered doors and window frames had forgotten what a coat of paint felt like. But this had once been an elegant part of the city, and stylish people had lived in it. You could tell that by the flights of steps that led up to the porches, and the stone urns and knobs and pineapples that decorated the gateposts — the house at the further corner had a pair of stone lions, dozing with their chins on their paws and their tails tidily laid alongside. Many of the hall doors had pillars on each side of them, some of the windows sported iron balconies, crooked and rusting, and some had little panes of colored glass set into them, near the top. And at the top of the steps, beside each hall door, there were metal brackets for scraping the mud off your shoes (so old Mr. Harrison had told him) when the maid came to answer the peal of the brass bellpull.

But the doors lay open all day now, and there were no maids and only holes in the plaster where the brass bells had been. And a house that had been large enough, fifty or sixty years ago, for one family, now had seven or eight families living in it, in two or three or four rooms apiece, and the sour little trampled gardens reminded Matt of the hen run on the farm they had left behind them in the country two years ago, only that the hen run was better. Nothing had survived in the gardens except the toughest grass and a few tall spindly bushes that were too prickly to be swung on and too thin to be climbed. And one of these, because it was early April, had put out impudent sprays of blossom, right at the top, like a bunch of colored feathers on the head of a withered old Indian.

"There are too many cats already," Mrs. McGinley said.

Certainly there were plenty. From where he stood he could see two of his own protégés sparring and squealing on the top of a wall before they disappeared. He hoped they'd fallen off. But this evening it seemed to Matt that it wasn't cats there were too many of, but people. And smells from suppers and the same bouncy tune coming from three or four radios at once. But people most of all.

There was Madge from the house next door; she'd been washing her long straight red hair, and was sitting with it spread out, like seaweed, on the railings that divided his flight of steps from hers, and knitting under the tent that it made. There was Sidney, the Jamaican boy, slipslopping in gym shoes, on the paper route that he did after he got home from school, shying the right papers into the right porches, and halfway to the next door before they'd landed. Sidney's dad drove a bus, and sang to it; if you were in the front seat sometimes you could hear him. There was Eddie coming up the basement stairs with the Probation Officer who'd called round to see him. Eddie had been caught pinching at Woolworth's, he'd been lying low a bit since. There were the Flint twins fighting together on the pavement as usual, because their mother's long arm wouldn't allow them to fight inside the house. There was a whole tribe of the Flints, all with the same pale hair that was almost white. Mostly they went around in a tribe and nobody liked them very much. There was old Mr. Harrison being fetched in from the chair where he sat beside the gate on days that were fine and warm. His daughter, who was a dressmaker and whose sewing machine purred from the room on the ground-floor front of Matt's house, was holding his arm and he walked very slowly with a smile on his white polished face, and slid his slippers scrapily along the path.

The Probation Officer was shaking hands with Eddie. Probably he was saying, "Good lad." Eddie was looking serious, he always looked like that, you'd wonder how he got himself caught. There was Henry, the silly clot, coming home from choir practice with his hymnbook tucked under his arm, looking pious, as if he didn't get paid for being a chorister in the Cathedral. He must have bought himself a Nuttycrunch on the way home, his cheek was full and moving. Nuttycrunches were sixpence. It wouldn't do his bad tooth any good; he'd have to tell about his bad tooth one of these days. There was Henry's young brother, the Trailer, mooning about on the steps. Everywhere Henry went, except choir practices, the Trailer had to go with him. Now he'd seen Henry and had tagged on. Henry took no notice of him, he never did. It was like having a shadow, other people saw it more than you did. There was Gwen, looking holy and mooning about on her roller skates because this wasn't her night to trot off to the Mission and sing hymns. She was always very rude and scornful about Henry, who got paid for singing hymns. But she got a Christmas Treat out of the Mission and a day at the seaside in the summer.

Mrs. McGinley pulled the plug out of the sink, and the water, screeching as it always did, began to whirl round and slide away. The cat was startled and jumped off the sill, aiming for the top of the bay window of the room below. Where it went from there Matt couldn't see. But it had gone, the view from the window was gloriously free of cat. The water gave a final guggle and Mrs. McGinley wiped the sink and twirled the dishmop.

"There! I told you it had somewhere to go! You're too soft, Matt. That animal can look after itself. It's what we've all got to do, isn't it?" She looked pink and pleased, because she'd won.

"Oh I'm going out," Matt said, deciding suddenly that it was all too difficult.

"Out? Where? What about your lessons?"

"Just out," he said and was already halfway down the stairs with the door slammed behind him. He heard it

11

open again when he was in the hall and knew she was looking over the banisters, but he backed against the wall and waited until the door closed once more. Then he crossed the porch and went through it.

"Hallo, Doormatt, who's been walking about on you?" Madge said, staring at him through her hair.

"Ha ha," he said, "very funny."

"There was a moth-eaten old cat around looking for you. Did you know?"

"So what?" He tried to catch hold of a piece of her hair to pull, but she jabbed at him with her knitting needle and he made his escape.

"Hiya, Matt!" the Flint twins shouted, calling a truce, but he didn't bother to reply. Henry sang at him "Lo, who is this that cometh?" very chocolaty and nutty, and the Trailer waved, but he took no notice of either of them. He narrowly missed getting tangled up with a skipping rope as he turned along the street and Gwen, who was doing some dreamy turns on her skates, nearly ran him down and then lost her balance and collapsed on the pavement looking surprised and indignant, with the wheels of her skates still turning. "Boys are awful," she said, "but I'll forgive you." He said, "Don't strain yourself," and she put out her tongue and he ran. He had to get away. It wasn't cats. It was people.

He had reached the right angle of the Square and turned up it — or he was just going to until he saw on the pavement, ten yards ahead of him, the cat, the Dragon cat. There was no need to wonder what it was doing, it was simply waiting for him. Meanwhile it cleaned its paws and stretched out a hind leg further than seemed possible and cleaned that too. Mrs. McGinley's windowsill was so very dusty, it seemed to say. And it waited, for Matt.

It would have found Matt too, had it not been for a dog at the other end of the street that was occupying a tenth of its attention. This gave Matt a split second in which to escape. But where? He'd just got away from all that crowd, he'd no intention of turning back. There must be a place somewhere where he could be by himself, unlooked at, unheard, unneeded, untouched, away from eyes and elbows and voices. Just a place that was empty except for himself.

And so, for the first time in the two years that he had lived in the city he turned, not down a side street away from the Square, but into the deep tangle of trees and bushes that were fenced in by railings and made the Square's center. Not that this was empty — the jungle was so thick and dense that it looked as if, but for the railings that bound them, the trees and bushes would have burst right out and spilled across the street. But these railings were stout and very close together, so close indeed that it had never occurred to Matt that it would be possible to get to the other side of them, and he could not now have done it except for the fact that at the particular spot where he had halted two of the railings had been forced a fraction apart, so that there was space, or might be space, for a body that could wriggle and wasn't too fat and that didn't mind getting well scratched when it reached the other side.

He was thin, he could wriggle, he didn't mind. He entered the leafy darkness gratefully and headfirst, so that if the cat had turned in time it would have seen no more than the soles of his shoes. And now he was alone. No pair of eyes, cat's or human, could reach him here. This was an extraordinary feeling, one that made him forget how his knee had hit a stone as he came down, and that the disturbed city bushes had filled his eyes and mouth with dust.

He lay panting, and stared through the bare lower branches of the trees to where the buds, big with leaves, made a pattern against the outer air. It was quite dry here. Leaves from last autumn and the autumn before and autumns before that again had lain where they had fallen, undisturbed by wind or children trailing their feet through them or by the road sweepers' brushes. They made a deep substantial carpet.

He enjoyed being completely alone. Spiders don't count, he told himself, collecting a couple of them off his face, neither do birds, as a fussy hen blackbird squawked in panic above his head. Higher up in the branches a larger bird stirred and grumbled; perhaps he was trespassing on the private territory of the owl whom he heard at night if he lay awake until the traffic noises stopped. So that's where you live, is it, he thought. That tree is yours.

When he had recovered his breath he turned back towards the world that he had left. It was interesting to see it like this, spread out in one piece, and surprising how different it looked, like staring from the inside of a goldfish bowl into a room that you thought you knew very well but that didn't look the same at all.

He could see all the houses on his side of the Square at once. He could see Madge and Henry and the Trailer. Henry was rubbing his cheek, so his tooth was talking. He wondered what Eddie had found to say to the Flint twins. Now Gwen's big sister's latest boy friend, who had come up the street, had shooed the twins off and was talking to Eddie, very close, holding his arm and smiling. Eddie didn't smile. This was because his arm was being privately and expertly twisted, Matt could see that from his hidden viewpoint. Then he saw Sidney's dad, Mr. Lumba, very large and dark, standing at the window of his room doing his arm-stretching exercises and stopping to scratch himself, while Mr. Ricardo, two floors down and one house to the right, had leaned over the balcony and was singing "O Sole Mio" in a lazy tenor voice that lifted sweetly above the street noises. Now Mr. Lumba had heard him and opened his window wider to listen, and was joining in with a bass accompaniment of his own invention. "O Sole Mio," sang Mr. Ricardo. "Diddy boop, diddy oompa Boop!" commented Mr. Lumba. They had heard each other now, and were making a pattern out of it, and enjoying themselves.

Gwen's big sister was collecting a sheaf of pink stockings that had been hanging on a string across the window to dry. Mr. Harrison appeared briefly in his window, wearing stripy pajamas and smiling and twiddling his white fingers at the budgie in the cage. Now

Miss Harrison had come to draw down the blind. Soon the sound of Miss Harrison's sewing machine would fill the stairs, often Matt heard it still busy long after he had gone to bed. Now Matt's mother was coming down the steps with a bag of washing for the Launderette. If Matt had been at home this would have been his job, but he had become so much apart from everything that it didn't even occur to him. Mr. Ricardo looked down and saw Mrs. McGinley and he smiled and put his hand on his heart, but she went past quickly with her head bent though she must have seen him. "O Sole Mio!" repeated Mr. Ricardo, very sad and sentimental. "Boddy boddy oompa Boop!" added Mr. Lumba. Matt's mother spoke to Madge, whose hair had paled to brick color as it dried, and went on down the steps.

When she had gone Matt turned and started to inch his way towards the center of his territory, following what seemed to be a tunnel in the undergrowth. Was it a tunnel? Anyhow, it was possible to travel along it on hands and knees, and after what seemed a long journey the light increased and the bushes and trees stood at arm's length from each other and he was able to stand upright and look around.

He was close to the church. He had never seen the church before, except for the top of the tower which was visible from the window of the landing on the floor above his mother's kitchen. He knew it was there, of course. The landing window had pieces of blue and red glass set in the corners, and he enjoyed the way the tower became blue or red in a blue or red landscape, when you squinted through the colored panes. There was a new church now, built in the Housing Estate at the end of the bus route, and some people went there, but most of Dove Square cleaned their cars or lay in bed or took the dog out or did the washing on Sundays, and this church had been shut up for years and years.

The entrance to the churchyard had been through gates on the further side of the Square, the side where the warehouses were. The gates had chains and padlocks on them, and they were spiked like the railings, only more so, and no one ever thought of climbing them to explore. But here he was now, on the inside of the churchyard.

There was a small clearing of grass in front of the church, and the grass had crept into the gravel drive that ran round it and disappeared, smothered with branches, in the direction of the gates. Trees on each side of the church pressed closely against its windows. Most of the windows had boards across them that reached halfway up. And over the double doors of the church, as if to hold them more tightly closed, ivy had stretched its wiry fingers.

It was through these doors, fifty or sixty years ago, that all the ladies and gentlemen who lived in the houses in Dove Square had come, when church was over, and they had walked down the drive and out of the gates and climbed the flights of steps to their hall doors and gone in to eat their Sunday joints. And if the drive had been wet and soft they would have used the footscrapers to take the mud off their boots and shoes. Old Mr.

Harrison had been a houseboy in Number Five, helping the butler. Sometimes he would talk about it. "The style of them!" he would say. "The glossy top hats and the feather boas and the bowing that went on — it would take you to the fair! And golden sovereigns on the collection plate as common as half crowns!"

Matt stretched his hands out and pressed them against the solid stone of the church. He was surprised that it felt warm — sun-warm, as if the place was alive after all. How strange to be so near his own world and so cut off from it, in this silence. Even the sounds that he could still hear — the buses and the tune of the ice cream van and the voices calling and an ambulance braying its way up the main street — made his silence deeper. The sun was sinking, glinting through shifting leaves and dazzling his eyes. Time I was going home, he thought. But I'll come back.

He found the entrance to the tunnel and was diving into it when he heard the blackbird again, this time louder and more urgent. Cats, he thought, cats about. She's got a nest somewhere with fledglings and that's why she's creating such a racket. Cats? He was right. One cat, a cat he knew, a striped, smiling cat, stepping out of his own private tunnel as if it owned it. To Matt's surprise the animal took little or no notice of him except for the briefest of nods ("Haven't we met somewhere?") and then continued in the direction of the church.

Matt turned back to watch. On the further side of the church there was a part of the building where the roof was lower and the windows smaller, with frosted glass in them. It was this that the Dragon cat was making for, making in fact for one of these windows whose upper part was open, so that a well-judged leap and a quick scuffle on the sill took the animal over and in, without even a backward glance to see if Matt was interested.

He should, of course, have left it there, have turned and gone home, but curiosity and a prickling indignation that the cat owed him something more civil in the way of goodbye made him follow it, by way of a convenient drainpipe, onto the windowsill, through the window, and into the room inside.

It was dingy, dusty and smelled of damp. It was the room where the church committee used to meet, but only a rubbed piece of linoleum on the floor showed the pattern where the legs of the chairs and the table had stood. There was a high fireplace with the remains of a bird's nest lying in it, a long cupboard, two doors, a drift of withered leaves in one corner, and no furnishings except a framed picture which hung crookedly over the mantelpiece of a clergyman with whiskers clamped to both his cheeks and a dog collar so high that he must have been standing on his toes to see out.

"You don't half look silly!" Matt remarked to the photograph, and the clergyman stared sadly, as if he agreed.

It was a dreary place, but the Dragon cat didn't seem to think so. It curled up in one corner, as if it had arrived home, and prepared for sleep. "So this is where you live, is it?" Matt said, and the glorious idea broke over him that if one cat lived her then two cats could, three — perhaps a dozen cats, and a number of other lost and homeless creatures too, so that all his housing problems might be solved.

"I'll sneak some milk and an old coat for you, Dragon," he promised, and with this happy intention made his way outside again and edged his journey home along the tunnel.

The tunnel was dark, but Dove Square was full of lights, the tall streetlights, the sliding lights from the traffic, the winking oranges of the zebra, and the many-colored pattern from the lighted windows of the houses. He reached the railings and, after a careful inspection of the street, slipped through them.

It was only as he stepped back on the pavement that he had the uncomfortable thought that whoever it was who had taken the trouble to bend the railings just that necessary distance apart had almost certainly taken the trouble afterwards to go through them, and that someone as well as himself knew both the inside and outside of Dove Square.

2

Old Mr. Harrison died before morning. He had been sitting in his chair at the gate just the evening before. Once in the night Matt woke and wondered what time it was. The city streets were still, so still that he heard the clock from the University striking three; a ship coming up the Channel on the full tide hooted, and then the owl called, imitating the ship. Matt lay awake thinking of the bird that flew over the rooftops while he was in his bed and that was hidden snug in the tree while he was at school. Then he heard voices on the lower landing and doors were opened and closed. His mother's door creaked and he knew she was out of bed and on the landing, listening.

"What is it?" he called. "What's happening?" but she came tiptoeing into his room and put her hand on his shoulder and told him to go back to sleep, so he didn't know about Mr. Harrison until the morning.

She told him at breakfast. "Are you sure? Who told you?" and she said she'd heard them talking last night.

"Didn't you go down?" he asked, but she said, "What good would that have done?"

"It would have been friendly."

"Miss Harrison has her own friends," she said, and

buttoned her mouth the way she did when it wasn't any good going on.

Next day after school the children talked about it, soberly, scuffing their feet through the weeds in the garden.

"Poor old Mr. Harrison," Henry said.

Gwen said, "I don't see why poor," aggravatingly cheerful like she always was, and knowing more than the rest of them, with her holy face on. "He'll like heaven."

"He was perfectly all right with his budgie," Henry snapped at her, and Madge began to laugh and they felt fidgety and peculiar, as they had done since they'd heard about it. They hadn't spoken to Mr. Harrison very often, but he'd always been there, sitting in his chair at the gate, him on one side of it and the laurel bush on the other, when the days were fine, or at the window beside the budgie's cage if it was wet. They couldn't see the budgie now because the blind had been drawn down until after the funeral, which was to be on Saturday. People from the Square usually died in hospital. The children missed the sound of Miss Harrison's sewing machine, and slipped past if they met her in the porch or on the landing, feeling they should say something and not knowing what. They wished the funeral could have been any other day except Saturday, so that they would have been away at school.

"No need for you to hang about," Mrs. McGinley said to Matt on Saturday when breakfast was over. She had pulled the curtains across the window. The room looked peculiar with the daylight trying to come through.

"Where shall I go?"

"Anywhere," she said, gathering up the dishes and not even offering him any messages. So he went downstairs and found Madge and Gwen and Henry and the Trailer, squatting in a huddle at the foot of the steps, as if they'd been swept out with a broom. None of the Flints were there and there was no sign of Eddie. Eddie and the Flints were ganging up these days.

"That makes six wreaths," Gwen counted as a man arrived in a van and carried the flowers up to the door. "I think wreaths are lovely."

"I bet you won't get six. You mightn't even get one," Henry said and Gwen grew pink and Madge said "Shut up, you" to Henry and the Trailer looked as if he was going to cry. Then Sidney arrived with his dad, who was magnificently smartened up and wearing a black tie that made him look quite different, and Sidney tagged onto the children while his dad went up the steps.

Mr. Lumba stopped when he got to the top and noticed them and said, "Is this a committee meeting or something? Why don't you kids all clear off somewheres?" and then Mr. Ricardo in his black tie joined him and agreed, "Yes. Why don't you?" and they went into the house.

"Well, why don't we?" Matt asked. Since Eddie had gone over to the Flints he often found himself taking the lead. But nobody seemed to think moving was a good idea.

"Go? Where?"

"There's the library."

"Standing room only in there on a Saturday morning, you can't even get room to blow your nose."

"The Baths?"

Nobody had any money for the Baths.

"The Downs, then?"

"Too far."

It wasn't as far as all that and they wished they were there. Nobody wanted to stay but nobody could decide to move or where to move to, as if they'd got weights on their feet and cotton wool for brains.

"This is a lousy sort of a Saturday morning," Henry said. "Hasn't anybody got any money?"

Madge confessed that she had, but it was for fish. "Cod for Cousin Maudie," she said.

"Better go and get it, hadn't you?"

"I don't want to."

This needed no explaining, nobody liked being sent for fish. Mr. Taffe, the Fishmonger, when he fixed you with those eyes of his, could make you go right over, like the Hypnotist at the Panto, or put a spell on you the way he'd done with Mrs. Ellis from the corner, who'd gone in to buy a couple of whiting and come home, so people said, with three pounds of the best salmon steaks.

"He makes me come on all over queer," Madge said, plaiting and unplaiting the end of her hair very quickly without looking, "but then I'm psychic."

"If you mean you're a nut case," Henry said — "anyway, give us the money. We'll use it for you." But

Madge closed the hand that was holding it tighter and shook her head.

Gwen was shocked. "She couldn't. It isn't her money."

"Girls!" Henry snorted.

"If you didn't spend so much on Nuttycrunches," Madge snapped at him, "we could have taken a bus somewhere or something." She had noticed that Henry's tongue was busy inside his cheek. Trust Madge to notice. "You'll have to tell about that tooth sometime," she scolded.

"It isn't hurting."

"Of course it's hurting. Anyone can see."

"If you can see you ought to be sorry for him," Gwen said, "you're never sorry for anybody," and Madge laughed and said, "Nobody's ever sorry for me."

"Mind your own business anyhow," Henry growled, and Madge teased, "Cowardy, cowardy! Going to the dentist's nothing."

"Bet you yelled the place down when you had yours out."

"I did not yell!"

"You did so!"

And a thin prim lady in a black coat and hat who was going up the steps said, "SSSh! Don't you know your manners at a sad time like this?" very fiercely at them sideways, so that they felt terrible.

Then big Mr. Lumba came out onto the top of the steps again and said, "Hi! You kids there! Are you deaf or lost the use of your legs? Hop it! Like I said! And quick!" and when no one moved he put his hand into his pocket and pulled something out and threw it at Matt and said, "Here, you're the biggest. Maybe this would help. Now get going!" and he went inside again.

It would have helped, quite a lot. It was half a crown. There was time for them all to see it shining as it spun and fell, before Matt's hand went out to snatch for it. And they heard the noise it made as Matt's hand missed it and it fell on the flags and rolled very neatly down the grating in front of the basement window.

Nobody said anything. Things had gone down that grating before. Once down they were gone for good. There was a treasure mine down there, and now an extra half crown added to it. Six fares up to the Downs or down to the docks, and something left over to spend when you got there. Or five Nuttycrunches to be bought at the corner shop and split and eaten slowly lying under a tree in the Park, or on the swings, perhaps, leisurely licking, or hanging over the bridge watching the trains. Or five comics that could be read and swapped over and read again. Matt knew they were all staring at him. Nobody told him it was his fault. Nobody needed to.

"Oh all right," he said, feeling hopeless. "Come on, then."

"Come on where?"

"I'll show you."

"But where?"

"Somewhere you haven't been before."

"A mystery tour, fancy!" Madge said nastily. But they

followed him and he led them along the street until he was level with the gap in the railings.

"Stop here," he ordered. "This is it. Are you ready?"

" 'Oh for the wings of a dove!' " Henry said, "and for my next trick — "

"Oh shut up, all of you. One at a time, no pushing or hurrying, and quietly does it," and he stepped through the railings.

He thought he heard them gasp as he entered the tunnel. And they all stepped into it after him, Henry, the Trailer, Madge, Gwen and Sidney, one after another, as smooth as beads falling off the edge of a table when the string of a necklace breaks. And because everyone who was in Dove Square on that Saturday morning was occupied with old Mr. Harrison's funeral no one noticed that they had gone, or how, or where.

Bang goes my secret, Matt thought dismally as he led the way. Bang goes being alone. There were only two days that I had it to myself. I'm soft, she says I'm soft, and she's right. And if I'd caught that half crown I would still be the only person who knows about this, the tunnel would still be mine. He reached the clearing and straightened and stood waiting for them to emerge.

One by one they came, stretching and disentangling themselves from the bushes, with sticks and pieces of leaves and spiders' webs in their hair and mouths, and such expressions of respectful surprise on their faces that Matt thought the sharing of the secret had almost been worth it.

"Gosh!" breathed Henry, fishing down his neck for a spider that had got away. "How did you find it?"

"How long have you known?" Madge asked, unwinding a twig that had got tangled up in her hair and then losing patience and yanking a bit of her hair off with it.

"Exceedingly wow," said Sidney. He never talked much, but what he said was always very polite. "Oh very nice and most pleasant, I'm sure." And his face brightened into a wide smile.

Gwen said, "Isn't it gorgeous?" and the Trailer sat down on the grass, pulling at the daisy buds and making pleased noises.

And then the cat arrived, stalking across to rub itself against Matt's knee and someone asked, "How many more of them have you got hidden away here, Matt?" and Matt said, "Hundreds and hundreds," and they sprawled about on the grass, laughing longer than the joke lasted because it was so pleasant to laugh and have space to laugh in.

Matt introduced it. "This is the Dragon."

"Hiya, Dragon!"

They lay on their backs and tickled the Dragon's neck while he walked about on them. The sky had become overcast and was a curious green color.

"It's going to rain," Henry said. "Another ten minutes and it'll come tipping."

"Then we'll go inside," Matt said.

"Inside?"

Matt got up to lead the way. "Up here and through." He showed them the drainpipe and the window and they followed him one by one into the committee room.

If it had looked shabby in the evening light it looked shabbier than ever now. The walls were flaked and patchy with damp and everything was covered with a sort of gritty dust.

"Right dreary sort of a dump," Henry commented. "I don't wonder the Reverend Robinson Crusoe is looking a bit depressed." He jerked his head towards the photograph of the whiskery clergyman. That was like Henry, unimpressed because he hadn't been the one to show the secret place to the others. "What else is there to see? We may as well look, when we're here."

They found that one of the doors opened with a bit of coaxing and led into the main porch of the church. "Come on." Now they were standing just inside the big double doors leading outside. The keyhole of these doors was empty and when they squinted through they could see green buds pushing against the outside and a piece of sky beyond. Ivy had splayed out below the door and was spreading along the floor at their feet. There was a collection box on a hook, and Henry shook it but it was empty. There was a tired-looking mat on the floor. Otherwise — nothing.

"Quite a place — every mod. con.," Henry said, sarcastic.

The doors from this porch into the church itself were securely fastened. No amount of pushing or rattling did any good. But there were glass panes along the top. "Give us a leg up. We can look, anyway," Henry said, climbing on Sidney's back.

Madge had discovered some carving along the wall of the porch. "Look — writing!"

"What does it say?"

She rubbed her finger along it and blew, clearing the dust. Then she read out, " 'The Church of St. George Without.' "

"Go on, what's the rest of it?"

"That's all — 'The Church of St. George Without.' "

"There must be more."

"There isn't."

"Without what, please?" asked Sidney, and Henry who was still on his back said, "Without quite a lot, if you ask me. Come and see!" And they took turns on Sidney's back.

There wasn't much to see inside the church and even if there had been they wouldn't have been able to see it, because most of the windows had been boarded up, almost to the ceiling. They could make out stone walls, stone pillars and a high arched roof, but no pews, no lights, no pulpit, no furnishings. It looked forsaken and down-at-heel.

"But it must have been beautiful once," Gwen said in her holy-holy voice.

"It's a right dump now," Henry declared, "not like a proper church at all."

Then Gwen fizzed up and said he should know, getting paid for going to the Cathedral, and that you didn't have to have stained glass and all sorts of fancy trimmings for a church to be a church, and Henry barked back that you had to have a bit more than four walls and a lot of spiders and a smell of damp, if you asked him, and Madge said nobody had, actually, and the Trailer, when it was his turn to come down off Sidney's back, landed on the cat's tail, and the cat let a screech out of him and frightened the Trailer who began to cry, and Sidney said, "Please not to cry," and when this didn't do any good Gwen told the Trailer you couldn't cry in church and Henry said why couldn't you, and Gwen said if he didn't know there was no sense telling him, and Henry said people cried at funerals, didn't they, and they were reminded again of old Mr. Harrison, and called a truce.

It was during this truce that they heard the noise. It was an irregular scraping kind of a noise and it seemed to come from somewhere over their heads.

"What is it?"

"Shut up! Listen!"

"Someone's there!"

They listened. The noise continued. It was certainly coming from up above. *Scratch — scratch. Scra — a — pe!* Once there was a long slithery kind of a clatter and a short silence and a bump and someone said "Ouch!" and someone else said, "Try again, clot!"

"Someone on the roof," Matt said.

"Who?"

"We'll find out."

Matt set his eye close against the big keyhole in the outer door and was surprised to find that all the scenery was eclipsed by a close-up view of what seemed to be the leg of a pair of jeans, swaying. Matt had a thin metal ruler in his pocket. He threaded it into the keyhole and poked briskly. There was a yelp and the sound of tearing cloth. The jeans disappeared. He told the others.

"But who was it?"

"I couldn't see. Only his jeans."

"We'll go and find out."

"Quietly does it."

They crowded back into the committee room and had a whispered committee meeting, ten times as quick as any that the Reverend Robinson Crusoe had ever presided over.

"Back through the window the way we came," Matt decided. "And take cover in the bushes until we're all through. After that scout round to the front of the church and see who it is."

They liked the idea. "Up St. George!" said Henry, who was first through the window. "St. George and the Dragon!" Madge said, diving after him. "Why a Dragon for St. George please?" Sidney asked and Matt said, crouched under a deep canopy of sprawling laurel. The "Tell him, someone," but nobody had time. They were through the window briskly, one after the other, and rain had begun, thin threads that seemed to hang in the air before they fell.

Matt formed them into a file. "I'll go first. You behind me, Henry. Then Sidney. The girls and the Trailer in the rear." Madge made a face at Matt but didn't argue. They edged their way round the corner of the church until they could see the ivy-draped porch and the steps that led to the entrance doors.

A stepladder was propped against these doors. At the

bottom of it a boy lay nursing his shin which showed white through the torn leg of his jeans. Another boy steadied the stepladder. A third was spread-eagled against the sloping roof of the porch, his feet in the gutter, his hands clutching for and just missing the crest of the slates. Someone else had already managed the climb and was leaning over, encouraging him.

"Who are they, please?"

It wasn't surprising that Sidney asked because each figure had a stocking drawn over his face, so that his hair and ears and nose were flattened.

"Do you know who they are?" Matt whispered to Henry. Henry shook his head. "Never seen them before. Or — maybe."

"They've got a nerve!"

Gwen said, "What do you suppose they're doing?"

"This is our place, anyhow," Henry said, suddenly deciding that he belonged to it.

The climber's hand had reached the crest of the roof, and he hauled himself up and over.

"That makes two up and two on the ground," Matt decided. "Now's our chance! Get the stepladder out of the way and the rest is easy! Are you ready?"

They were itching ready. It was raining now in earnest and the sound of the heavy drops hitting the leaves was exciting, like the sound of drums.

"Come on, then!"

They stepped out from the laurels into the open, into a sudden sliding downpour of rain, and made for the intruders, whooping as they went. Madge and Sidney collared the ladder. Matt and Henry, with the Trailer

hopping around and squeaking, captured the two boys
who were on the ground. They were taken completely
by surprise and hadn't a chance. Matt sat on his
prisoner's chest. From the roof the two other boys, who
had been joined by a third as yet unseen, yelled insults
and defiance. The two captives pinned on their backs on

the ground yelled back, while the rain fell into their swaddled mouths and ears and eyes. Gwen, who had been circling round, suddenly swooped down on Matt's prisoner.

"I thought it was!"

"What do you mean?"

"We should have known — look!" She dodged the kicking feet and pounced suddenly to peel the drenched and sticky stocking off the prisoner's face. His hair, released, sprang up at once into the pale familiar tangle. Of course! One of the Flint tribe! The second stocking, removed, disclosed another.

"And I'll bet that's Eddie up there!" Matt called, pointing at one of the faces on the roof.

"It is! It is! And two more of the Flints!"

Lightning flashed across the sky. Eddie and the Flints ducked but not soon enough. They had been recognized.

"We know who you are! Come down! We've got you!" Henry yelled.

They came down, quicker than Henry expected, launching boldly out from the roof of the porch, and landing, through branches, on the grass not many feet away, and the battle began in earnest. Madge and Gwen took over the places on the chests of the wriggling captives, while Henry and Matt and Sidney went for the newcomers and the Trailer held onto the stepladder. Thunder grumbled and rolled and crashed, and the rain, having held its breath for a moment, came down thicker than ever, and then eased again to allow the lightning to split the sky.

"Like the Wrath of God!" Gwen shouted, bouncing up and down on her prisoner's stomach in her delight and appreciation.

It was a pity she bounced because it gave her prisoner the chance, between bounces, to roll sideways and scramble to his feet, dragging at Madge and so releasing the other prisoner. He dived for the stepladder and tore it out of the Trailer's hands. Henry and Matt and Sidney left their private battles to help, but they couldn't do it; in any case the enemy had had enough and the retreat was on.

The rival gang had apparently entered from the far side of the Square, negotiating the spiky railings of the main gates and then fighting their way through the overgrown drive, and this was the escape route that they chose now, pulling the stepladder behind them to give them rearguard protection.

If it hadn't been for this Matt and Henry, who were in the van of the pursuers, would have had a chance to catch up on them, but the stepladder, as it went ahead, dragged back the thinner branches of the trees and bushes, and then released them full in their faces so that they were whipped, blinded and drenched all at once, and by the time Matt came within sight of the gates three of the gang were over it, and the last two, with the stepladder precariously balanced between them, were just easing the seats of their pants delicately over the top of the spikes.

"Why on earth are they bothering with the stepladder now?" Henry said to Matt. "Why don't they drop it?"

"I expect it's Ma Flint's. Would *you* drop Ma Flint's stepladder?"

No time to discuss it. Matt, Henry, the girls, Sidney hoisting the Trailer, lost no time in following across the spikes and they were soon down the other side of the gates and had alighted on the pavement, breathing hard.

By this time Eddie and the Flints were rounding the next corner of the Square, still hampered by Ma Flint's stepladder.

"Quick! Quick! After them — we'll catch up on them yet!"

"Yippee!"

"Wolla wolla wolla!"

Any instructions that Matt might have tried to give

them were lost in the thunder. Anyway, they didn't
need instructions. Down the slippery pavement across
which lightning and rain took it in turns to skim they
ran, yelling, waving and whooping, with water spurting
from their shoes at every step. By the time they came to
the corner and turned it they had made up a good **ten**
yards on their quarry.

"Come on! Come on!"

They came on, skidding through puddles.

It happened that the people who had been to old Mr.
Harrison's funeral, and had come back to Miss Harrison's room afterwards for a cup of tea, were now
crowded in the porch and at the top of the steps, shaking
hands with Miss Harrison, waiting for the weather to
ease and give them a chance to scatter, talking quietly
and politely to each other, trying not to feel impatient
with the sad occasion which they all felt had gone on a
little too long. They were startled by a drumming of

feet that grew louder and nearer, by cries of anger fear delight and vengeance, and by a stampede of wild excited children, steaming like a herd of cattle, mud-streaked, with wet hair and clothes plastered to their faces and backs.

They poured along the pavement and across the road, and then drew up, halted suddenly with a stepladder swinging between two of them, gaping at Miss Harrison and at their parents, remembering suddenly what had been going on outside the railings of Dove Square while they had been occupied inside.

3

MATT was surprised to see his mother among the astonished and scandalized mourners who were leaving old Mr. Harrison's funeral. He didn't recognize her at once, partly because she looked different in her best coat and hat, partly because it was the first time he'd seen her in the company of her neighbors. Usually she went about on her own and somehow happened not to see people unless she bumped into them. But here she was, self-appointed to the outraged reception committee.

The adults and children stared at each other in frozen silence, and then like a light switched on the sun came out, shining brilliantly on their embarrassment and providing them all with a reason for moving.

Miss Harrison gave a final smile and slipped into her room. As soon as the door closed Mr. Lumba stretched out an arm and secured the scruff of Sidney's neck, Ma Flint seized one of her twins in one hand and her stepladder in the other. Henry and the Trailer were quickly hemmed in by relatives; Madge's weird Cousin Maudie, who had got herself up in deepest black with an eye veil like the Beautiful Spy, claimed Madge. Eddie's mum reached for Eddie and Gwen's aunt sidestepped and closed in on Gwen with a skillful flank attack.

Surprisingly it was Mrs. McGinley who spoke.

"You'll go to apologize to Miss Harrison," she decreed. "Tomorrow afternoon would be the most suitable time." She was addressing Matt but the other adults nodded, making it a unanimous verdict. "About half-past four," Matt's mother said.

When adults ganged up solid like this there was no sense in asking for justice or arguing which side had been to blame. In any case there were no longer two sides. When Mrs. McGinley passed sentence she had united them and from now on they were all in it together.

It was this uncomfortable knowledge that kept them apart through the rest of Saturday and during Sunday morning. They slunk around, avoiding each other, going into hiding with aged comics or devising solitary games and such private occupations as would make the time go by without too much thinking. But at twenty-five past four on Sunday afternoon Matt in his best clothes, uncomfortable and clean, found himself outside his door and on the way downstairs, and saw that Henry and the Trailer, Madge, Gwen and Sidney were already spread uneasily about the hall, keeping as far from each other and from Miss Harrison's door as they could. They closed in on Matt. They were all looking queer. Gwen's nose was pink, she had been crying; Madge was in a blind fury with her lower lip stuck out and chewing hard on a tail of her hair while she blew a tune through her teeth. Henry looked like a nervous commercial traveler on his first day selling vacuum cleaners, and the

Trailer shadowed him so closely that none of him really showed. Sidney's solemn black face would have been funny on any other day but this.

No one spoke until Henry said, "We can't."

"There isn't anything else we can," Matt growled, raising his eyes to indicate the houseful of heartless parents and relatives all snug behind their Sunday papers with their feet up.

"Where are the others, then? We're not going without them."

"You bet we're not."

Eddie looking bored with the Flint tribe behind him came tricking up the steps and the two gangs converged, jostling for position. Matt and Eddie were pushed to the front until they were standing shoulder to shoulder with their noses a few inches from Miss Harrison's door.

"You knock."

"No. You."

"It doesn't matter who knocks," Henry said wearily from the rear, "it sounds just the same, whoever's doing it."

A door on an upper landing opened questioningly and after a few moments was softly closed.

"What do we say?"

"We're very sorry, Miss Harrison. We didn't mean to make such a racket when there was a funeral on," Henry suggested.

Gwen recited, "We should have had more consideration and respect, Miss Harrison, in your time of deep sorrow."

"Very rude and ill-mannered to rampage. Not the thing at all. Please kindly excuse," came from Sidney.

They all contributed the little pieces in which they had been rehearsed. It seemed they had quite a lot to say. The impossible was possible now that there were words to it. A clock from upstairs struck the half-hour. "Zero," Henry said. Matt lifted his hand and knocked.

They heard a chair pushed back and her footsteps approaching the door. They watched the door handle turn and saw the door open. There was Miss Harrison. She looked first at Matt and Eddie, inquiringly, and then at all the other faces.

"Well!" she declared, and her thin-nosed face grew pink. "Well! This is a surprise!"

Matt felt himself prodded cleverly in the backbone and the first words were jerked out of him. "Please, Miss Harrison, we came to say we're very sorry — " and then his tongue dried up in his mouth and no amount of prodding would have produced another syllable.

"Oh, I was sorry too," Miss Harrison agreed.

"Rushing in a mob the way we did — " Eddie said.

"I know," Miss Harrison agreed, "such a pity! If you'd only been just a little earlier! But it was nice of you to hurry."

Henry's voice was lifted croakily from the rear. "So we thought we'd better come along and explain — " and he too faded out, in spite of Madge's elbow, which was busy on his ribs.

"How very friendly!" Miss Harrison declared. She smiled and opened the door wider. "Come along in.

Sunday afternoon can be very dull, don't you think? We'll put the kettle on. I was wondering what in the world I could do with all that was left. Nobody eats nearly enough at funerals."

Surprise made them dumb again and carried them across the threshold. The door closed behind them. From his cage at the window the budgie piped, "Hallo hallo hallo, company is it? Who's this, then!" but they felt too stunned to respond. Anyhow Miss Harrison kept them busy. A tablecloth to Madge, a kettle ("Go and fill it") to Sidney, cups, saucers, plates, a sugar basin and teaspoons to Matt, Henry and the rest of them, and milk for the Trailer to pour carefully out of a bottle into a jug with painted roses ("We'll be grand since it's a party"). And then from a cupboard a procession of cakes, biscuits, scones, cookies, brought from a stack of tins and boxes and set out on plates on the table, with dishes of butter and pots of jam.

"Well, this *is* nice!" said Miss Harrison when everyone had found chairs. "Reach for yourselves, all passing strictly forbidden, and it's your own fault if you starve."

No one starved. No one talked much either. Henry told Matt afterwards that if he hadn't been so surprised he could have eaten twice as much, but as it was he didn't do badly. Miss Harrison at the teapot grew warmer and pinker. They were all hungry because with this visit ahead of them they hadn't had much of an appetite earlier in the day for their Sunday dinner. Each plate, as it was cleared, was added to the pile of empty plates in the middle of the table, and the pile grew

higher and higher until the pattern on the tablecloth was visible all the way around.

"No more," Henry said at last, leaning back carefully with a glazed look. "I couldn't. Honest."

"Nor me."

"Nor me, Miss Harrison, really."

"It's been lovely," Madge said and actually smiled.

Gwen's busy conscience was still niggling. "You see, we thought you'd be mad with us, stampeding in like that."

"It was funny, wasn't it?" Miss Harrison agreed, setting down the teapot that was really empty at last. "How Pa would have enjoyed it!"

The budgie chuckled and they got up stiffly and went and wiggled their fingers at him. "He's glad to be back at his own window." Miss Harrison said. "I kept him in the kitchen because it was too gloomy for him in here, with the blind down. But he likes to see the street, don't you, boy?"

"Yeah, yeah, yeah!" agreed the bird.

"He picked that up from the wireless," Miss Harrison explained. "Pa used to say 'At least the budgie's with it, though that's not my idea of singing.' "

"I didn't know Mr. Harrison was fond of singing."

"Well, he should have been! He was fifty years in the choir at St. George Without."

They all froze when she said that. Madge's elbow reminded Matt that he was spokesman.

"That's the old church you can see in the trees inside the Square, isn't it?" he asked carefully. "It's a funny sort of a name — 'St. George Without.' "

" 'Without,' used to mean 'Outside,' " Miss Harrison explained. " 'St. George Outside.' "

"Outside what?"

"Outside the city wall. You see, the church was built years and years ago, when the city was quite small and a wall ran around the city to defend it against enemies. You can still see a bit of the old wall on the far side, the warehouses are built against it. And as the city began to spread and life became safer they built the church there and called it 'St. George Without.' "

"Was this all country then?"

"Green fields and woods, it's hard to imagine," Miss Harrison said.

"How long has the church been shut up?"

"It was the night the windows were blown in during the war that finished it. But even before that there were only a handful of people that used to go. Fifteen was a crowd, we used to say. But in the old days, before the other war, St. George's was crowded every Sunday. Pa

48

said you had to be a quarter of an hour early if you wanted to get a seat. And all the gentry who lived in Dove Square attended church morning and evening, regular."

"Who used to live in this house, Miss Harrison?"

"The four Miss Tomlinsons had it, the whole of it, mind you, to themselves — and a cook, of course, and two housemaids and a parlormaid and a manservant. When Pa was a boy he used to deliver the milk here — that was in old Colonel Tomlinson's time. Before six o'clock, winter and summer with the milk, and in his bare feet."

They looked out of the window at the flight of steps, trying to imagine it, but Miss Harrison said, "Oh no! Not that way! The milk went round to the servants' door, up the alley."

"Where did you live, Miss Harrison?"

"There was a row of little houses where the super-market is now, ours was the one at the end. They were all pulled down to make room for development. Our kitchen would have been bang in the middle of the cold meats counter."

"Was it a nice house?"

"Two up and two down and a cold tap," she said rather cryptically, "but convenient for church when you went three times on Sundays, like I did when I was a little girl."

They were silent, trying to think about Miss Harrison being a little girl.

"That was when the Reverend Mr. Robinson first came to St. George's," she added.

There was a gleam in Henry's eye as he nudged Matt. "What did I say? The Reverend Robinson Crusoe!"

"Tell us more!" they demanded, and she told them while they cleared the table and packed into the tiny kitchen and those that were near the front helped with the washing up.

"I wore a navy blue dress with braid on it," she said, "and black woolen stockings, and in the summer white lacy socks and a hat with daisy chains on it held by an elastic under my chin — I used to chew the elastic — and my penny for the collection inside my cotton gloves. One of the Miss Tomlinsons was our teacher — Miss Ada it was — and she gave us texts with colored pictures and gold letters when we knew our answers. She had a feather boa in the summer and a muff in the winter and she smelled of moth balls all the year round. There was Sunday School in the morning, then church, then more church in the evening and sometimes choir practice after that."

"You must have learned a lot," Gwen said respectfully.

"Let me see." She hung out the dishcloth on a string above the stove, and they went back to the sitting room. "I learned the Ten Commandments and the Catechism and a List of the Kings of Israel and Judah and how to find my way through the minor Prophets — "

"Obadiah Jonah Micah Nahum Habakkuk Zepha-

niah Haggai Zechariah Malachi!" Gwen gabbled, showing off and enjoying it.

"That's right. It makes a lovely noise, don't you think? And I learned how to sit still even if my clean vest was scratchy — I was a martyr and it was made of horsehair — and I taught myself games to play with the colors in the stained-glass windows, and I invented quick escape routes if either end of the church caught fire, and I cultivated the taste of wet elastic" — Miss Harrison's tongue came out for a moment, as if she was looking for it — "and how to make patterns on my hand by pressing the penny tight. The new pennies with Edward the Seventh on them were much better than the old worn ones with the Queen. And I learned that a church can be empty even if it is packed to the doors with people, and that sometimes — " Miss Harrison paused, she wasn't seeing them any more.

"Go on!" they said.

"Sometimes, even if the congregation was rattling in the pews, a church could be crowded."

"Crowded with what?"

"Angels and Principalities and Powers," she said, "and organ music battering the ceiling and waking up the stone faces at the tops of the pillars — "

"Are there stone faces? We didn't —" but one of the senior Flints kicked his younger brother skillfully into silence.

"Go on, Miss Harrison."

"At Christmas," she said, "the church was full of the smell of frost on hay. And at Easter — "

"Tell us about Easter."

"Light everywhere! Full of light and crazy with daffodils. But the best service of all was on St. George's Day."

"April twenty-third," supplied Henry, who kept a diary and knew that sort of thing.

She nodded. "That's right. On St. George's Day we had a special service and there were banks of flowers on all the windowsills and a flag flying outside on the flagpole, and the trumpeters from the Barracks were up at the back of the gallery — "

"Trumpeters?"

"Six of them, in their uniforms. Like six giants. You should have heard the noise when they joined in the special hymn that we sang at the end of the service, every year the same. All the stops out on the organ and everyone singing their heads off and the trumpets from the back of the gallery playing a tune of their own, like a ladder, high above the voices."

"We play bugles," the Flint twins said, "in the Scout Band."

"What was the special hymn, Miss Harrison?"

" 'Ye gates lift up your heads.' "

"You mean — to the tune of 'St. George's Edinburgh'?" asked Henry.

"Of course. St. George's tune. Do you know it?"

"We sing it at the Cathedral sometimes. It's a good one; all those Hallelujahs at the end!"

"Five of them."

"And the organ! And the bugles!"

Sidney stood up unexpectedly and put his head back,

52

and with his lips pushed forward sang "Root-a-too-toot-TOOT!" like a bugle, and then sat down again, and though it didn't make any difference on him you knew he was blushing.

"Just like that," Miss Harrison agreed. "By the end of the last Amen I was floating about in the air with my head bobbing against the roof — we all were. They had to pull us down by our ankles."

They nodded, believing her.

"And we had a Sunday School trip to the seaside every summer," she said. "The gentry lent us their carriages. I'll show you the photographs."

She pulled photographs out from the back of a drawer and spread them out over the table. Some of them were faded to the color of tea stains, but they were able to identify Miss Harrison as a small girl under a large hat. All the girls and the ladies were wearing hats. "There's Pa!" Miss Harrison cried, and there he was, with his bowler held on his knee and six inches of watch chain showing across his stomach. "And there's Miss Ada Tomlinson." With a feather boa round her long neck, because it was August. "And there's the Reverend Mr. Robinson!" Not so much whisker and looking jollier than he did on the wall of the committee room at the church. "And there's Mrs. L'Estrange, she always brought her little dogs!" And there were a lot of other people whose front doorsteps they now walked on though they had never heard their names before, or seen their faces.

"Who's the character in the sailor suit and long stockings?"

"Oh that's Theo Taffe — he was always a very tiresome little boy!"

"You mean Mr. Taffe who sells fish?" She nodded and they inspected him with awe.

"And there's someone else you know," Miss Harrison declared, pointing to a young man in a striped blazer and straw hat, with a most impressive pair of moustaches.

They stared, but couldn't guess. "Who is it?"

"Don't you know? It's Charlie Frick, of course!" Miss Harrison smiled fondly at the moustaches. "He was our solo baritone. Surely you recognize Charlie Frick?"

"You mean — old Shaky Frick?"

Everyone knew Shaky Frick, though there didn't seem to be any resemblance between this splendid young man and the shuffling figure in the raincoat who allowed himself to be towed round the Square three times a day by two Pekinese on leads. These were the dogs Mrs. L'Estrange had when she died, and she left them a legacy, and a legacy to Mr. Frick to look after them — he had been her gardener. The dogs were worth pots of money, and as they picked their way sniffily along the pavement you could see they knew it. "If you held them up by their tails, half crowns would fall out of their mouths," someone had told Matt and he still half believed it. They called Mr. Frick Shaky Frick because his head wobbled a little as he walked, in a kind of pattern, as if his neck was loose. The dogs (they were

54

called the Duke and Duchess) wore jackets when the weather was chilly, and sometimes they teased Shaky Frick by coughing, or going off their food for a day or two, or drooping their tails, which made him anxious because if anything happened to them there wouldn't be any more money coming in for him. So he always took very good care of them and listened to the weather forecast to find out whether they ought to be wearing their coats.

"Shaky Frick is an unkind name," Miss Harrison said, gathering the photographs together briskly. "He was hurt in the First War, that's why he's like that." And the children felt awkward because often when grownups talked about the wars you learned that people you made fun of were heroes and you ought to be feeling grateful to them.

"He used to ride on an Indian!" Miss Harrison announced and the children gaped.

"He what?"

"Surely you've heard of an Indian motorbike," she said, as if they were very ignorant. "Dear dear! Sometimes I rode on the back of it behind him — but I never told Pa. Charlie was studying to be a bank clerk, but when he came home from the war, gardening was all he was able for."

"Tell us what happened after the war?"

Miss Harrison put the photographs in the drawer and closed it. "Things weren't ever the same. Factories and warehouses and shops began to spring up round the Square, and the people who lived here said the air was smoky and the Square was noisy and they moved to new houses much farther out of the city, and for a while they came in to church at St. George's, in their motorcars, but as time went on fewer and fewer of them came, and the Reverend Mr. Robinson was growing old and couldn't get out to visit them, so they went to new churches nearer their new homes, or they didn't go at all, and the Reverend Mr. Robinson and Pa and five or six families were all that was left. And the big houses in the Square were let out in rooms and flats — that was when we moved in. Pa never thought it was natural, us living in the Miss Tomlinsons' dining room, but he liked it because even after the church was closed he could still see it from the window until the trees grew too tall."

"Tell us about the church being closed."

"Well, you see in the next war there was this bomb — it landed where the cinema is now — and most of the windows of the church were broken, so they boarded them up, and later on they took away the pews and the furniture and the fittings and the organ — everything that would be useful in a new church. Except the bell, they didn't take the bell."

"A bell! We didn't know there was a bell!"

"Just a small one. But they said it would cost too much to move at the time and afterwards I think they forgot about it. Funny, it was a long time before I got used to doing without that bell. I did everything to it — putting on the potatoes and filling the hot-water bottles. It was never the same without it. Sometimes in the last year or two the Reverend Mr. Robinson would have to ring the bell himself and then run round and take the service — and no one there but Pa and himself. And then they'd lock up and come home. You know I always said Pa ought to have done something about those keys."

They leaned forward. "What keys?" they breathed.

She jerked her head towards a hook beside the fireplace. A bunch of keys hung from it. "The keys of St. George Without. Pa brought them home the night they closed up for the last time, after the workmen had been in to take what had to be taken. He never knew who to give them to, because the Reverend Mr. Robinson was taken ill and went to Eastbourne to live with his daughter, and nobody ever asked for the keys. I said the Bishop should have had them, but Pa said 'If he wants them let him ask — he's welcome. Meanwhile they're in my charge and there they'll stay.' "

"And the Bishop never did ask?"

"No." She lifted the bunch of keys on her fingers and let them swing from the key ring, then she set them down in the center of the table. They stared. Matt could hear Henry's fingers moving hungrily inside his pockets, it was so quiet.

"I worry about those keys," Miss Harrison said.

"Which key is which?" someone asked.

She told them. The largest of all the keys, the handsome one with the decorated haft, was the one that unlocked the large entrance doors into the porch; the next biggest, but with a plain haft, was for the side door into the committee room and vestry, and the next size was for the boiler house, and the one that was like it, but smaller still, was for the door of the stairs that led from the porch to the belfry.

"That little door — I wondered — " Gwen said and turned raspberry color. "Clot!" said Henry under his breath, and Gwen squeaked as his shoe got her on the ankle.

"Miss Harrison," Matt said, "what about the doors from the porch into the church — I mean, I suppose there would be doors there and they would be locked, wouldn't they?"

She showed them a key. "That's it. At least, that's one of them."

"You mean — there's another?"

She nodded ."That's the key I worry about most of all."

"Why?"

"Because it's still there."

For a minute there was silence. Henry gulped and said, "What do you mean? Still where?"

"Well, you see, I used to go over to the church on a Friday evening to do the dusting, so that it would be spick for the weekend, and Pa left the side door open for me, because that was the night he was over cleaning out the clinker from the boiler and doing the rest of the jobs. But he had an extra key made so that I could get from the porch into the church 'So that we won't need to go chasing after each other, Queenie,' he said. 'But keep it somewhere safe.' "

"And you did?"

She nodded.

"There's a loose piece of plaster just behind the collection box on the wall," she said. "I tucked it in there tied to the little key of the harmonium — because I played the harmonium for the Sunday School in those days. It saved carrying it about and I was afraid of losing it; so that was where I kept it. The day the church was cleared I forgot about it until everything was locked up with Pa's keys when the workmen had gone away, and I never dared tell Pa that it was still there. But I always had a feeling someone ought to do something about that key."

Matt heard Henry's whisper, "They will, sister, they will!" and echoed it silently.

Gwen said, "I didn't know you could play, Miss Harrison. Do you play the piano as well?"

"I used to," she said, growing rosy pink and blinking, "a little. Off and on. Not now. Not very often."

"Play for us now," they demanded.

They opened the piano and led her to it. She took the vases and mats and photographs off the top and sat down, protesting and pushing her hair back off her face.

"Please!"

"Shall I? Oh — I don't know."

"Go on," they urged.

"What shall I play?"

They crowded around. "Play us St. George's tune."

She played it, fumbling at the notes until she found the right ones. "Sing! Go on — Henry knows it too!"

"Come on then, Henry!"

So Henry and Miss Harrison sang. Miss Harrison's

voice was quavery and a little off-key and Henry's true and reedy as a flute, hitting every note just where he wanted it:

> *Ye gates lift up your heads, ye doors,*
> *Doors that do last for aye,*
> *Be lifted up that so the King*
> *Of glory enter may!*

"Then it's the tenors and basses," Miss Harrison said, thumping with her left hand and putting on a man's voice:

> *But who of Glory is the King?*

" 'The Mighty Lord is this!' " piped Henry in reply, and they joined each other in the final lines:

> *Even that same Lord that great in might*
> *And strong in battle is!*
> *Even that same Lord that great in might*
> *And strong in battle is!*

By the time they had reached the second verse most of the others were joining in, shakily at first, and at the end of the verse Miss Harrison and Henry steered them through the five Hallelujahs and the three Amens.

"It was better with the trumpets!" Miss Harrison sighed.

"Be the trumpets, Sidney!" they demanded.

And they did it again with Sidney being the trumpets and it sounded much better.

"I suppose we ought to go," Matt said when it was over. "That was smashing, Miss Harrison!"

"It was, wasn't it?" she agreed, and opened the door for them, and they all shook hands with her and she went back into her room.

"Well!" they breathed, keeping the brake on their excitement though the door was closed, "what next?"

"Do you think she knows?"

"Knows? How could she know?"

"The way some of you were talking," Eddie said in a tone of disgust, "you were shouting it out loud."

Gwen began to say something and stopped.

"The thing is," said Henry, "when do we go and collect that key?" It was the question they all wanted to ask.

"We've got to be careful or we'll muck it. Nobody must know."

"Do you think they guess? I mean, when we came back all leaves and mud. What about the stepladder? Did she say anything?" Matt asked the Flints.

"She said a lot but she didn't know where we'd been with it."

"All the same," Matt advised, "we'd better give it a week to cool, just in case."

"A *week?*" Who could wait a week?

"It's been there for donkey's years. It'll still be there."

"Matt's right," Eddie agreed. "Anyway there's not

much daylight after school and Saturday can be tricky. Sunday would be best."

They nodded. Sunday, then.

"Everyone go separate," Matt directed, "and watch it. Nobody's to see us getting in — nobody. You must melt through the railings, understand?"

They nodded again.

"Sunday, then. Half-past four. And meet at the top of the tunnel."

Matt's mother squinted at him over the mending when he went in. "Well?" she inquired, as if she was Mrs. Daniel and he'd come back from paying a call on the lions. "Well?"

"Well what?" Matt said.

She looked puzzled. "You were there a long time, weren't you?"

"Were we?"

"She understood, did she?"

"Oh yes. She understood."

"And I thought I heard singing."

"Oh yes," he said, playing it as casual as he could, "we were singing."

She waited for more and then bit her thread in an exasperated way and said, "I've had my tea."

"And I've had mine."

"You've —"

"We had tea with Miss Harrison."

"With — ?" Her scissors slid and fell off her lap.

"It was a real smashing tea," he said, "plates and plates!"

4

IT was bad luck that Sunday was sunny and fine, one of those peerless days in April that make you remember what summer is going to be like and itch for it, a June day that has got into the wrong place in the pack. So in the afternoon the people in Dove Square were gathered at their doorsteps and open windows and in their bits of gardens, sampling the warmth, finding reasons to talk to each other and be lazy and sociable.

If it had gone on raining, thought Matt, watching them from his mother's window, they'd all have been inside and safely glued to their tellies, with the door shut. But Mr. Lumba was stretched on the grass at the gate with a newspaper on his stomach and his hands clasped across it, one eye open to all that was going on, and Mr. Ricardo, who was coming in with a pile of clean tablecloths and tea towels ready for next week at the Restaurant (he took them to the Launderette that stayed open on Sundays), had stopped to talk to Mr. Lumba. Madge's weird Cousin Maudie had put on a playsuit and extended herself in a deck chair trying to sunbathe but Matt could see the goose pimples on her from where he was standing, and Ma Flint was actually having a joke with Gwen's aunt, probably about

Henry's father who was cleaning his car. "The dirt on his car is all the dirt a man ever sees," Ma Flint said.

"What are you doing, Matt?" called Mrs. McGinley from the kitchen, and he said, "Looking out of the window," feeling irritated with her because she hadn't gone outside and with everyone else because they had. But trust her to be different. He had nothing but admiration, however, for the way the disappearing act was going into operation out in the Square.

Gwen, idling with her skipping rope, had dropped it to attend to her shoelace just opposite the gap in the railings, and the next minute the pavement was empty and Gwen was through. Henry, coming back from evensong, smug and blessed (the Trailer shadowing him) melted into the tunnel without hesitation just as a Post Office van crossed over it. Madge, who was bouncing a ball a few yards further up the pavement, waited until the ice cream van trundled by, playing "The Bluebells of Scotland" and while everyone's attention was drawn to it she and her ball followed Henry. Sidney was mooning around the stationer's, fiddling hopefully with the cigarette machines. Shaky Frick and his little dogs came past and a roving mongrel made insulting remarks at them and the dogs said, "Charming!" in very BBC accents and while Shaky tugged at them and the mongrel pranced around making very low and vulgar replies all eyes were turned on what could become an interesting dogfight and Sidney took the chance, crossed the road and was gone.

Then came the Flint tribe and Eddie, all in a bunch,

and stopped dead opposite the gap. "They're going to muck it," Matt thought despairingly, "one at a time I told them — silly clots!" But they weren't so silly. It was hard to see how many Flints there were because someone had pinched someone else's cap and there was a general dust-up with everyone milling round, jumping and snatching, and little by little the crowd thinned, though no one could have seen how, and then the cap went high into the air and landed on the mail box on the other side of the street and everyone watched it coming down, and by the time Eddie had gone across to collect it the pavement was empty. And when Matt had gone down the stairs and through the front door there was no sign of Eddie.

A passing bus gave Matt the cover he needed, and when he reached the grass patch at the end of the tunnel he found the company assembled, sprawled in two camps, Eddie and the Flints a little apart from the others. The Dragon, who was sampling one knee after another, made straight for Matt and crouched in busy adoration over the couple of sardines he had brought in an old envelope — he had saved them from tea.

"I'll bet your pocket stinks," Henry said. "Anyway, what are we waiting for? Let's go and get it." There was no need to state what "it" was.

Matt said, "Just a mo, there's something we'd better decide first." They said, "What d'you mean?" and shuffled closer, hugging their knees.

"In a way," Matt said, "she gave it to us."

"Most kind and elegant lady," Sidney said, "she sure did."

"That is, of course, if it's there," Eddie corrected.

"Of course it's there!"

"How do you know?"

"We can soon find out!" They got up, itching to go.

Matt stopped them again. "If it's where we think it is, then after we've — used it, it goes back where we found it, and nobody — nobody touches it again until we're all here together."

"Meaning who exactly?" Eddie asked in a nasty way.

"Meaning anybody, idiot." Matt wished Eddie and the Flints hadn't been in on this, it would have been more comfortable without them. "What do you say?"

Eddie looked at the Flints and they nodded.

"All right then," Eddie said, and Henry said, "It'd better be," and the junior Flints put out their tongues and made rude noises at Henry, wiggling their fingers at the backs of their ears.

"Anyhow, have you and your lot been inside?" Matt asked, and Eddie said no, they'd only been on the roof.

"Why the roof?" It was obvious that Henry had made up his mind to be awkward about Eddie.

"Why not?"

"Looking for birds' nests I suppose," Henry said, "or studying The Sky at Night?" and Eddie said, "Well, what were your lot doing inside — saying your prayers?" and Gwen said, "Oh shut up, you two!"

"It's going to be a fat lot of use if you fight all the time," Matt said. "Are you going to stick to the rules or aren't you?" And Henry and Eddie glared at each other and said of course they'd stick to his flipping rules and who did he think he was anyway? Solomon or something?

Matt said, "That's all right, then," and Gwen snorted, "Boys!" and moved quickly out of Henry's range.

"We know where one key is anyway," Matt said; "at least we think we do."

"We know where the others are too."

"Yes, but we can't get them."

"Oh I don't know," Henry said, rubbing his nose in an aggravating kind of way. "It could be done."

"What's that supposed to mean?" Eddie asked.

"Nothing."

"You did mean something."

"Well, it might be easier for some of us than others — I mean if you've had any practice at that sort of thing."

Eddie went bright red and two of the Flints got up and went for Henry, and Gwen and Madge unexpectedly uncoiled and hauled them off, and someone pulled Madge's hair and there was a general schemozzle until things got sorted out again. But the air seemed to be clearer after that, and when Matt said, "Come on then, if you're coming," they fell in behind him like a string of lambs, and Henry and Eddie gave each other advice on the best way to get through the window into the committee room. From his frame on the wall the Reverend Robinson Crusoe stared at them with alarm and dismay. "Don't get excited, old boy, or your whiskers will short," Henry told him. "It's all right — we're on your side."

From the committee room they moved into the porch and formed a rough semicircle round the collection box which hung in its place on the wall. "That's it. That's where she said."

No one moved. Now that the moment of truth was so near they were afraid to hope.

Matt said, "Come on."

"A loose piece of plaster, she said, on the wall above the box."

They moved closer. "Who'll look?"

Matt and Eddie were shoulder to shoulder in front but someone said, "Let the Trailer do it! He's the smallest!" and the Trailer was pushed out from Henry's shadow, looking pink and pleased and all at once a separate person.

"Go on!" they urged, and he stepped forward and stood on tiptoe, reaching up the wall.

"He's too little! He can't reach!"

"He's just the right size!" Madge cried and she seized him and hoisted him up. "Now! Try now!"

His short fingers traveled over the stonework, poking and prodding for the loose piece of plaster. But he couldn't find it; the stone was hard and solid and had no secrets.

"It's no good!"

"Higher! Try higher!"

He tried higher, and nearly outreached himself and grabbed at the wall, and they whistled with tension as

something came away in his hand — plaster and frag-
ments of stone, dust and cobwebs, falling on the flagged
floor, but among them something that rang out when it
fell and they knew it was metal and yelped, "The key!
The key!"

It was Matt who stooped to pick it up and blow the
dust off it, and he held it in his extended hand while
they all stared. It was indeed a key. He closed his fingers
over it, pressing its hardness into his palm.

"Now for it," he said, and they turned in a body to
the doors that led from the porch into the church. Here
Matt who was in front paused and shoved the key over
to Eddie, for no reason that he could think of except
that it seemed drafty, being in front so much, and he
said, "Go on — you do it!" So Eddie took the key and
put it into the keyhole where it fitted sweetly and he
turned it, and Matt and he put out their hands to push,
and the doors creaked and swung open.

They went in holding their breath, listening to the
sound of their feet disturbing the silence that had been
there since the evening many years before when old Mr.
Harrison had watched the workmen take away the furnishings of his church and had locked up for the last
time and gone home and hung his bunch of keys on the
hook where they had seen them hanging yesterday, in
Miss Harrison's room.

Although there was still sunlight outside, little of it
came into the church except at the top of the windows
where they were not boarded up, and here the beams of
dust-filled light made a kind of crisscross archway over

their heads. Below this the church was dark, and the first feeling Matt had was of disappointment for something he had expected to find and that wasn't there. He wondered if the others were feeling the same way because nobody said anything, but they came to a halt halfway up the aisle and their eyes gradually became accustomed to the dimness and examined what they found.

"Not very lively, is it?" Henry said.

"Well, what did you expect?"

"Oh I don't know." But you knew he had expected something.

There were two doors at the farther end of the church but both of them were locked so that was no good. Stone tablets on the walls had words carved on them, and Sidney shone his pocket torch while Henry read out the names of people who had died and how old they were and what their families and relations had thought about them.

"They can't have been as good as all that," Gwen said enviously.

"Well, you couldn't put it on a tablet if they hadn't been."

"Look! There are faces on the pillars — she said there were!" Madge cried, pointing. They craned their necks, and where the arches of the roof sprang from the top of each pillar they could see the faces, kings with crowns, warriors wearing helmets, bishops with their miters, and the faces of ladies with drapery scooped gently below their chins, and in the less important places were the

faces of animals, lions, bears, hounds, foxes, and highest up of all, where the arches met and crossed each other, were the angels' faces, with their wings, small and tidy, laid like open hands against their cheeks. Every face was different but they all stared down at the children with the same expression of empty-eyed surprise.

The Trailer, scuffing with his feet for a sweet that he had dropped, made another discovery. "Pictures!" he announced, and knelt down, pushing the grit and dust away with both hands, and soon they were all on their knees, grubbing with him at the colored mosaic on the floor, and discovering inch by inch a looped and scaly tail.

"A serpent! Is it a serpent?"

They pushed and blew and pulled out their handkerchiefs for the job, and spat and rubbed, and the picture became clearer; not a serpent but a lashing, threshing dragon with a wide, fanged mouth from which flames spurted and an eye rolled towards St. George, who had planted his mailed foot on a loop of the beast's neck before he thrust his blade home with both hands. And behind the dragon lay a miniature landscape, a hill, a castle, battlements.

"St. George! St. George!"

"There must be a Maiden in Distress somewhere," Gwen insisted. "Come and look," but the boys wouldn't, and Henry said that if she'd got herself into distress she could find her own way out of it, and Gwen said he was horrid and — and then they heard the voices, men's voices, coming from outside the building, and they prickled with alarm.

"Who is it?" Matt said to Eddie who was standing next to him, and he remembered afterwards the sick scared look on Eddie's face.

"We can see who it is from the room outside," Henry said. They crept back into the committee room and Matt was hoisted on Sidney's back and reported to the others.

"Four of them — smooth-looking types. Don't know any of them, at least I don't think so." The smell of adult tobacco accompanied Matt's report. "Having a good look at the place. Can't hear what they're saying. Shut up, the rest of you. No, it's no use, they're talking low. One of them is shinning up the drainpipe, hope he mucks his elegant pants, he's on the roof, he's up and over. Now two of them. Now the others. They've got torches."

"What do you suppose they want up there?" one of the Flints asked, and Henry retorted, "Well, what did you want?"

"We were only having a look round."

"That's what they're doing."

But they were doing more. Soon there were sounds of muffled hammering.

"Whatever it is I hope they won't be long," Madge said. "Cousin Maudie'll be wild. I said I'd be back to set her beastly hair before she goes to Bingo."

"Well, we can't shift till they clear off."

"Anyway, we've got to find out what business they've got here." Henry was talking as if he owned the place.

"They'll want to know what business we've got."

"They certainly have a nerve — I mean they're trespassing."

Nobody said, "So are we," but it dawned on them uncomfortably that they were.

"Perhaps they're Social Workers from the Mission," Gwen suggested brightly, "students, you know, fixing the roof."

"That isn't what they look like," Matt said, and Gwen, with a pious flavor in her voice, said it was wrong to judge people by what they looked like, and Matt snapped that she couldn't talk, she couldn't see them, could she, and Gwen said she could if she went through the window and why not go and ask anyway, what harm would it do, and Matt slid to the ground and said, "You wouldn't dare — or would you?" and Gwen grew pink and said she would, and Matt and Henry and Eddie and Sidney looked at her and at each other, deciding, and then Matt said, "All right. We've got to know, anyway, haven't we?" and the boys nodded, and they gave Gwen a legup through the window and listened holding their breath as she slid to the ground on the other side.

"Up Gwen and St. George!" Henry whispered and Matt told him to shut up.

"Hallo!" they heard Gwen say, and then, louder and squeakily, trying to make her voice carry, "Hallo, you up there!"

There was a pause in the banging, and a man's voice

said, "Look who's here!" and another, "What do you want, kid?"

"What do *you* want?" Gwen said. "I suppose you're Social Workers from the Mission," and one of the men laughed and said, "Yeah yeah, smart kid, aren't you? Got it in one."

"Fixing up the roof, are you?" Gwen asked.

"What's that?" one of the men called.

"She wants to know if we're fixing up the roof."

"We sure are." The voice sounded amused.

"You mean for when the place is opened up again?"

This must have been funny too. "Opened up is right." Then the man said, "Look, little girl, go away and make daisy chains. What are you doing here, anyway?"

"Yes, what *is* she doing?"

The mob inside the committee room listened yearningly for Gwen's reply and imagined they heard a small gulp before it came. "Oh, hadn't you heard? We're the Junior Choir practicing for the Opening." They could tell from her voice how pleased she was with this flight of imagination.

There followed some mumbled conversation between the men that the children couldn't catch.

"Would you like me to sing you a hymn while you're working?" Gwen volunteered. Oh she was doing it well, they could just see her, pie-eyed and smug.

"What's she saying now?"

"She says do we want her to sing us a hymn."

"Go away, little girl. Just go away."

"It's no trouble, really." The strains of "Brief life is here our portion" drifted in through the window, brave and a little shaky but very determined.

"You can join in if you like," she said, breaking off between verses, "you often sing it at the Mission."

There was no reply and the banging on the roof was resumed though with less enthusiasm.

"Crummy sort of words," Eddie commented, and Sidney agreed, "Most extremely sad." Gwen droned through five verses of eight lines each and had embarked on "Christian, seek not yet repose," when one of the men interrupted, "That was very nice, little girl. Now go away," but Gwen couldn't have heard him for she finished that one and launched out on "For those in peril on the sea" without pause or invitation.

"How long do you suppose she's going to keep it up?" Matt whispered, and Henry said that there were seven hundred and forty-four hymns in the cathedral hymn-book, including the Introits and Anthems, and Eddie said he couldn't wait for the Introits, and Gwen drew breath and commenced, "Take it to the Lord in prayer," swooping up and down luxuriantly wherever it was possible to find an excuse to swoop.

Something heavy was set down on the roof and a voice complained bitterly, "I can't take much more of this, can't you *do* something?" and Gwen broke into a rollicking tune in which the words "Rolling home on Jordan's tide" recurred again and again.

"That one isn't in the cathedral hymnbook," Henry sniffed snootily, but Sidney commented, "She has rhythm, she sure has rhythm," and slapped it out quietly on his thigh.

"Look, little girl," came a weary voice from above, "I thought you said you were with the Junior Choir."

Gwen interrupted the refrain and said, "That's right."

"Then where are the rest of you?"

"Inside."

Eddie sucked his teeth sharply as if he'd been hit; Matt heard him and wondered why.

"Well, don't keep them waiting. Go on in. Let's hear what it sounds like from there."

"Well, all right I will," Gwen agreed.

"And step on it, little girl."

There was a scrambling noise and Gwen's fingers gripped the windowsill and soon she slithered down among them, breathing hard, her eyes bright, expecting their applause.

"We've got to sing," she announced, "we're the Junior Choir."

Henry said, "That's your idea. Gosh, Gwen, you can't half tell lies."

"Lies?" Gwen looked shocked.

"Sounds as easy as picking raspberries, the way you were doing it," Henry went on. "Pity they couldn't have heard you at the Mission."

"Oh!" All pride went out of Gwen, like the air out of a pricked balloon.

Matt said, "Oh shut up. She only told him we were the Junior Choir."

"Which we aren't."

"Hurry up, you inside — let's hear from you," shouted a voice from the roof.

"If we don't sing they'll think we're just snooping."

"What'll we sing? We don't know anything."

"What we sang with Miss Harrison — you know."

"Do you remember it?"

"Bits. Do you?"

"Henry knows it anyway — don't you, Henry?"

"Where's that choir?" came from outside.

"Go on, Henry, start us up!"

So Henry started them, and they sang, "Ye gates lift up your heads, ye doors!" to the tune of St. George's Edinburgh. It was a ragged performance, none of them remembered it properly and but for Henry they would hardly have made their way through it. Sidney didn't help much either. He was working on a version of his own devising, swaying his head and clicking his fingers, and in between the lines when the rest of them were pausing for breath, he ejaculated comments of his own, so that the result was something like this:

" 'Ye gates lift up your heads, ye doors — ' "

"Come on now — wide'n high!" from Sidney.

" 'Ye doors that last for aye — ' "

"Get moving! — I say get moving!"

They staggered to the end of the first verse, and the second wasn't much better, and they left Henry and Gwen to tackle the Hallelujahs and the Amens, while Sidney did some highly original embroidery above and below and all round them.

78

"That was pretty lousy," Matt said, "the Reverend Robinson Crusoe is disgusted with the lot of us," and Madge said, "It would be better inside the church," and the young Flints said, "And we could bring our bugles," and Henry said it was all Gwen's fault, anyway, and Gwen said what else could she have done, and it was only after the squabble had cooled off that they remembered the audience on the roof for whose benefit they had been singing. Matt mounted on Sidney's back again and looked out.

"Well?"

"They've gone! Not a sign!"

"Are you sure? All of them?"

"Hopped it — the lot."

"Let's go and make sure."

"Maybe they're still snooping around," Eddie said. "Better to wait a bit."

"I knew they weren't Social Workers," Gwen grumbled.

"Then who were they?"

They went out through the window, Matt first, Eddie hanging back to the last. The men had gone.

"We must have scared them off, we were so horrible," Henry decided.

Darkness had been falling outside and it was time for them all to make their return journey. The tunnel was in black shadow, and the leaves of the laurels were dew-wet as they brushed against them. The sounds of the city came back to them. The owl, waking overhead, called inquiringly and Gwen squeaked from fright. One of the

Flint twins imitated the owl. Sidney said, "Not like that. Listen. I make." And he made, not the Christmas card version of the owl that the Flint twin had done — "Too-whit, too-whoo!" — but the tawny owl's true call, first a click in the throat and then, "Hoo, hoo, hoo!," like three smoke rings blown inside one another, and the owl replied to Sidney, and ripples of appreciation ran up and down the tunnel.

"Careful how you go when you get to the railings — pass it up!" Matt said to Henry; they were bringing up the rear. And one by one, cleverly, taking their time about it, they joined the world outside the railings and stepped into street light.

"Go on," Matt said, nudging Henry when only the two of them were left.

"Wait a mo. I want to talk to you."

"All right. What about the Trailer?"

"He's all right, Madge has got him."

They crouched together just inside the railings. The shadows of the railings made Henry's face stripy. He was looking solemn and important and when he moved the light glinted on his glasses.

"Well, what is it?"

"The gap in the railings — we'd have noticed it if it had always been here. So we know it wasn't. It was those chaps that made it."

"I daresay. But how?"

"I saw it once on the telly. You put a car jack in sideways, that bends them open. Easy, like wire."

"Very cunning, but — "

"If they took the trouble to do that then they did it for something."

"Yes I know. But what?"

"I don't know."

"We don't know anything about them anyway."

Henry's glasses flashed. He pulled something out of his pocket. He said, "There's something we know. I picked this up from the grass after we came out. Take a look."

He handed it to Matt. It was an empty cigarette packet. Matt turned it over. It was still an empty cigarette packet.

"Well?"

"Can you see it properly? Not a usual kind," Henry said. "Fancy, wouldn't you think?"

"Maybe they were expensive types. . . ."

"He looks an expensive type, don't you think?"

"What do you mean? Who?"

"Gwen's big sister's new boy friend. He smokes these."

Matt whistled respectfully through his teeth. "You've got something. I only saw his back, but that was who it reminded me of."

"But Gwen would have known him, wouldn't she?" Henry asked. "I mean, she would have said."

"She mightn't have known. She didn't say. You were too busy chewing her off for her to say anything. Maybe she didn't get a proper look at him. Anyway, he waits for her sister around the corner."

Then Matt remembered how he had seen Eddie talking to Gwen's big sister's new boy friend while he was waiting around the corner, or rather Gwen's big sister's new boy friend talking to Eddie, and the unpleasant way he was doing it. He had decided he wouldn't say this to Henry, not just then, when Henry asked, "Did you notice Eddie tonight?"

"What do you mean?" Matt said, marking time.

"You know! Dead scared. And afraid to go through the window till he was sure the coast was clear."

"He wasn't like that," Matt said, for the sake of argument.

"He was! You saw. And anyway, there's another thing."

"Well?"

"Eddie was up on the roof with those Flints, wasn't he?"

"So what?"

"Didn't you think it a bit odd? I mean — him playing kids' games, with a stocking over his face? Eddie? With the Flint kids?"

When you considered it, it certainly did seem a bit odd. But suddenly Matt thought of something else that put his niggling suspicions of Eddie right out of his mind. "Henry! I've just remembered!"

"What?"

"The key. I forgot it!"

"You *what?*"

"We were in the church, remember, and then we heard the chaps talking, and we nipped around into the committee room to have a look-see. And I forgot to lock up and take the key."

"Idiot!"

"I know," said Matt miserably.

"Where is the key, then?"

"Still there — in the keyhole."

"You are a nit, Matt."

"I'll have to go back and get it."

"Shall I come?"

"No. You go on."

"Sure? I'll come if you like."

"What's the good of two of us?"

"Well, all right then." So Henry ducked through the railings, and Matt listened to the sound of his footsteps diminishing on the pavement, and then, feeling that it had been Henry's evening, he turned again and entered the dark tunnel, by himself.

5

"IT's your own silly fault," he told himself as he made his way back, "you've only got yourself to blame." Not that this helped but it kept him moving. He wished already that he'd asked Henry to go back with him, but he was jealous of Henry because he had found the clue of the cigarette packet and had had the sense to realize what it might mean, and he'd spotted Eddie's behavior and suggested a reason for it. Henry'd been too clever by half and knew it. And Gwen had been quite smart with her hymn-singing act, although she'd been no good at all in saying what the men were like. And now he'd gone and left the precious key in the door. Well, that wasn't a crime, was it? Anybody could do it, and it was only a case of going back into the church and pulling the key out of the lock and everything would be all right.

In this darkness the difference between the outside-railing world and the inside-railing world was intensified. He felt very lonely, and the sounds from outside that still reached him — the voices, the soft swish-swish of cars, and the pattern of passing footsteps — only made him lonelier. Sunday evenings in Dove Square could be social. Mr. Ricardo opened for a couple of hours for fish suppers. He would be sliding the blinds up just about now. Matt imagined the warm comfortable smell, the lights and laughter, the music from the juke boxes. Sometimes Mrs. McGinley bought fish suppers on Sundays, and they carried them home and ate them out of their paper, like a picnic, in front of the telly, and perhaps his mother talked about the country and the house where Matt had been born, and about his father, not sadly, but like taking something good out of a drawer and looking at it, and knowing it would always be there when you wanted it again.

He reached the clearing and stepped out into moonlight, moonlight undimmed and uninterrupted by city lights, shining gentle and bland, as it had done at home on fields and woods. He went through the window easily, half expecting to meet the Dragon on his way to the night life of the chimney pots, but there was no sign of the animal. The old coat that Matt had thrown down in a corner was empty and when he put his hand on it, it was cold. Then on into the porch where the doors of the church still lay open, and inside them the pillars rose like the trunks of trees into a web of crisscrossing moonlight.

He was half afraid to put his hand out to the keyhole, but when he did so he found the key at once and drew the doors quietly together and locked them, and then slipped the key into his pocket and turned to cross the porch again, feeling pleased with himself and scornful of Henry. Of course the key had been there. Who would have taken it? It was like Henry to get het up about nothing. He would tell him so.

He had hooked his hand onto the window frame of the

committee room and was ready to jump and scramble through when he smelled cigarette smoke again, the same cigarettes, and he unclasped his fingers quietly and crouched, waiting. So the chaps had come back. They were outside.

He heard a voice. "All quiet. They've cleared off, like I said. We can take a quick look-see."

"Too late for much now. What were they doing anyway, the kids?"

"Well, you heard what she said."

"Did she invent it, that yarn about the church being used again? Nobody told us."

"And naturally the Bishop would have dropped us a line."

There was laughter at this and another voice said, "If the kid was on the level then it looks as if we've moved in just in time."

"The question is, how do we do it, with that little lot around?"

"The porch is easy, but it'll take a double-twenty before we can tackle the big stuff. And we'll need other gear, too."

"Call it all off. Too risky."

"Call it off nothing. Those kids were fooling us to-night. They'd no more business here than we had."

"They were a choir, she said."

"But did you hear them?"

"They sounded all right to me."

"And you would know!" This produced more laughter. Then — "How did they get in to begin with? I mean, right inside?"

"If they were a choir like she said then they'd have had a key."

"Had they a key? Anybody notice if the doors were lying open?"

"Not the big doors, anyway. The ivy would have been ripped off. We'd have seen it. Could have been a side door."

"My guess is the kids were fooling."

"You know something? We could do with those keys ourselves."

"What way?"

"Lock the kids out, to start with. Scare them off. Store our gear. And keep the stuff locked until we're ready to collect it — if it lies in the open then anybody who strays in here can see it. The place is getting too populated."

"The keys must be around somewhere. Someone must have had them when the place was shut up."

"Dan-boy could fix the locks, couldn't you, Dan-boy?" Dan-boy said he could. Easy. Leave it to him, he said.

"Better to have the real keys with us in case we're interrupted. 'Social Workers from the Mission, doing repair work, complete with genuine bunch of keys.' That kid put us on to something."

There was a murmur of agreement, then someone said, "The rest of the kids got in through the window, like she did. Look, it's still open. They didn't have any keys!"

There was a pause, then — "You're right, you know."

The shadow of an arm and a prodding hand were thrown against the pane. Matt crouched lower.

"Well, what about it? Shall we go in and take a look round?"

"Hardly our size, is it?"

"We could make it."

More shadows crowded onto the pane. Matt, with panic leaping in his stomach, looked round for shelter. The bare room had none to offer him — except perhaps the cupboard against the wall beside the window. No time to choose, no time to think. Shoes grated on the stonework, and the light from the window was obscured by a body. Matt went headlong for the cupboard and stepped inside. There was depth enough to take him. It smelled abominably. Hooks at the back of it prodded his spine, but he drew the door closed, triumphant at having found shelter.

The men's voices were muffled now, they seemed to have come no closer. He couldn't hear what they were saying. His own breathing in the restricted space rasped noisily, he tried to control it. Now his throat was full of dust, he would have to cough. He fought against this, and tried to hear what was going on. But nothing seemed to be going on; a sentence or two that was indistinct, then nothing. Silence. They had decided not to try the window after all and had gone away.

When he was sufficiently sure of this he pushed the cupboard door gently to open it. It was rigid and didn't yield to his hand. Something must have stuck. He pushed again, harder this time, and produced a metallic rattle that told him that the catch of the cupboard door, which had opened with the twist of a knob on the outside, had clicked tight and there was no way of opening it from the inside. He had made a prisoner of himself inside the cupboard.

It was easier to admit that he was frightened than to pretend that he wasn't, and since he was alone there was no reason for pretending. He was indeed very frightened. The fear caught him in his chest, like hands, squeezing. Once this had eased a little he tried to plan what he would do. Not that there was much to plan, not from inside a cupboard, but there seemed to be two choices. He found a toffee in his pocket and chewed on them and it. He could yell and thump the inside of the door, and perhaps the men might not have gone very far away and they would hear him and come back and let him out, but this mightn't be at all pleasant. Or he could wait until the morning and be discovered. Once word had got around that he was missing Henry would know where to look, and he would tell, and people would come and search in St. George's — the police, perhaps — and they would find him, and the secret would be known to everybody and everything would be spoiled, just in the opening of a cupboard door. So neither choice was any better than the other. He'd made a right muck of things. St. George would have been disgusted. Matt imagined Henry, solemn and self-important with the police, getting all the credit. Real telly stuff. Henry — again!

It was warm inside the cupboard and growing warmer and increasingly difficult to think, and since everything he had to think about was frightening or sickeningly disappointing he lapsed into a kind of dismal half-sleep, easing his shoulders between a pair of coat hooks.

The coat hooks hurt him as he jolted awake, hearing the footsteps and remembering where he was. There aren't any footsteps, he told himself, it's like a mirage in the desert, I'm only imagining them. But they continued and came closer, then there was a scrambling noise and now the footsteps were very close indeed, were divided from him only by the thickness of the wood of the cupboard door. Someone was in the room.

Easy now, take it easy. It's one of those chaps come back, trying to pull a fast one on the others, that's who, nothing to get excited about. Nothing. But the tread isn't heavy, like a man's tread, it sounds light and slippered, the way Sidney does delivering the papers in his gym shoes, but it can't be Sidney because he limps a bit since he got his foot flattened the time he was just a kid and the bread van started up when he was underneath it. So it isn't Sidney. But there are a lot of other people it could be.

The crack in the cupboard door wasn't wide enough to be any good; anyway it was dark. The footsteps had come past him, now they were going away. They mustn't go. *They mustn't go!* It's a long time till morning. And yet if it's one of those men — suddenly Matt realized that there was a way of sending a message that one of the boys only would understand, and he decided to take a chance on it.

He put his mouth to the crack of the cupboard and made an owl call, not the true call of the owl from his tree, but the way one of the Flints had done that evening, copying the owl the wrong way "Too-whit! Too-whoo!" very softly and breathily, so that if the person in the room was one of the men they might be deceived into thinking they'd heard the bird from his tree outside the window, and would take no notice, but any of the gang would recognize it as being produced by one of themselves.

The footsteps stopped, like a thread cut by scissors. Matt repeated the call, this time the "Whoo!" trembled. Someone outside the cupboard (was it Henry? It didn't sound like Henry) asked "Who is it? Where are you?"

Matt said "Here!" and scratched the inside of the cupboard door very gently with his fingernail. Footsteps crossed the room, the catch was turned and the door thrown open.

Matt stepped out. "Eddie!" he said. "Eddie! It's you!"

They stared, feeling each other's nearness, making sure of each other. There was just enough light coming through the window to see that Eddie's narrow face looked startled, as if it were mimicking his own. Then it relaxed and Eddie said, "What were you doing inside there? Playing Bluebeard's Wife or the Body in the Wardrobe?" and Matt said, "I wasn't sure who it was when I heard you," and Eddie said, "It wasn't a bad idea, actually, the owl, I mean," and Matt said, "Thanks, anyway."

He was glad it wasn't Henry, but he wished it hadn't been Eddie. He never felt comfortable and easy with Eddie, specially since he'd been up for pinching. Not that he minded him pinching particularly, but since it happened Eddie seemed to place himself apart from the rest of them, as if there was something special about him. When you talked to him he took meanings out of things that you hadn't intended, so that you had to think about what you were saying, not like with Henry or Sidney or the girls, where you just talked. Somehow Eddie could make you feel a kid, whatever you said, although he was thirteen, like Matt.

Eddie said, "What were you doing over here, anyway?" Matt, not wanting to be grateful to Eddie for longer than was necessary, explained about the key and how he'd come back for it. "I thought you were supposed to be looking after that key," Eddie said, and Matt said, "I was, that's what I'm telling you," and you didn't need any light to know that Eddie was smiling. So Matt asked, "What about you, anyway? What did you come for?" and Eddie just answered, "Lucky for you that I did, wasn't it?"

"Yes, but why?" And everything that Henry had been suggesting about Eddie came hotly back to him.

"Why not?"

"You know why not. No one was to come here alone, we decided that."

"You decided that."

Matt took a long, long chance that he would never have risked if he hadn't been feeling so angry. "Something to do with Gwen's big sister's new boy friend, I suppose?" and he knew, by the moment of silence before Eddie said, "Who?" that he was right.

He was feeling grand now, he knew he was on top, so he took another chance because the pieces of the jigsaw were beginning to click most happily together, and he said, "Dan-boy, isn't it?"

"Are you bonkers?" Eddie said, "Who is this boy friend of whoever it is, anyway?"

"The chap who was talking to you around the corner the other evening, you remember — the one who was twisting your arm." He looked sideways at Eddie, and wished he could have seen his face better because he would have enjoyed it just then. "He *was* twisting your arm, you know. Must have hurt you quite a lot."

There was silence. Then Eddie said, "I haven't told you anything. You can think what you like."

"Thanks very much, I'm sure. I suppose it was Dan-boy's idea that you should take a look round on the roof. It's the roof he's interested in, isn't it? And you took the Flints with you because it would look better if you were caught — kids playing Cops and Robbers or whatever sort of a game it was." And Eddie repeated, "I haven't told you anything."

"Whose side are you on, anyway?" Matt demanded.

"I'm sick of sides. It always has to be sides. I'm not joining up with anybody. Not any more."

"Those chaps came back this evening, they were here," Matt said, and felt the fear that ran over Eddie's face and said, "it's all right. They've gone now."

"Are you sure?"

"Dead sure. But I heard them talking. It's something to do with the roof. That's right, isn't it? And you know, don't you?"

"Do your own dirty work, Sherlock," Eddie said, and

was suddenly through the window, and Matt after him, into the clearing. Matt made the drop and felt Eddie's fingers closing on the soft part of his arm so tightly that it hurt. He was pulled in against the wall of the church. "I thought you said they'd gone," Eddie whispered, "you rotten liar."

"I — "

"Shut up!"

Eddie was watching something at the far side of the clearing. Matt followed his gaze, staring into the dimness, where a shape more solid than the trees and the bushes had separated itself from them. He began to laugh softly. "You idiot. Can't you see who it is?"

The figure was crossing the clearing now, had stepped out of shadow into full moonlight and became at once recognizable. There was only one person it could be.

"Now can you see?" and Eddie saw, and breathed with relief, "Shaky Frick! And the Duke and Duchess! What in all the world are they doing here?"

Shaky, preceded by the little dogs, picked his way towards the church, and when he had come within ten yards or so of it he straightened himself and stood to attention, clicking his heels, and the little dogs on either side of him froze, standing so still that the bells on their collars were silent.

"Corporal Frick and detachment reporting for duty, sir," Shaky announced.

"Who does he think he's reporting to?" Matt whispered.

"St. George, stupid, shut up!" Eddie whispered back,

and Matt was filled with a mixture of admiration and annoyance because Eddie had known and was right. The man and the two little dogs, solemn and slightly unreal in the moonlight, stood motionless except when Shaky's neck jerked, regular as a clock, pulling his head to one side a little and then returning it to its original position.

A twig snapped beneath Matt's shoe. "Who goes there?" Shaky demanded, turning towards the shadowed wall against which they were flattened.

"Boys," Matt confessed.

"Advance, boys, and be recognized!"

They left their cover and came towards him. The

dogs snuffed inquiringly and their tails registered satisfaction as they identified Matt. "So it's you, is it?" Shaky said.

"Hallo, Mr. Frick. We wondered what you were doing here."

"Routine patrol," Shaky said, "in performance of regular duties."

"Routine? You mean you come here every evening?"

"Nine o'clock, ack and pip emma, to be precise."

"Twice every day?"

"Unless acting under instructions to the contrary or if discretionary considerations make it inadvisable."

"But — why?"

"One moment." Shaky drew himself even straighter. "Parade — dismiss!" he barked, and saluted and unfroze, and the little dogs unfroze too and licked any part of Matt that they could reach while he rubbed them in the comfortable places at the backs of their ears.

Shaky loosened an imaginary belt. "Now that I'm off duty," he said, "I'll tell you about it, if you like." They sat down together in the clearing. "Somebody had to be detailed to keep an eye on the place and Corporal Frick's the man. The Bishop's very busy, you know. Of course I send in my reports to him regularly."

"You mean — you write to the Bishop?"

"Does he ever write back?"

"He will communicate in due course," Shaky said, "but things have to go through their official channels, you understand. It all takes time."

"How do you get in?" Matt asked. "Do you come up from the hole in the fence?"

"That? I should think not! That's an unsubtle bit of work, if ever there was one, very amateur. Only been there a few weeks. Somebody in a hurry. I informed the Bishop, of course. No, we have our own approach route, don't we?" and the Duke and Duchess rang their bells in agreement.

"Tell us how." You couldn't imagine Shaky and the dogs scaling the top of the high spiked gates.

"Is it safe? Is he One of Us?" Shaky asked, looking at Eddie sideways. Matt said he was, hoping he was right, and Shaky explained. "You know the row of telephone boxes against the far side of the Square. There's a gap behind them just wide enough for personnel to infiltrate, and a loose railing — shall we say a *loosened* railing? A simple maneuver, really. Nobody looks at Charlie Frick and his little dogs, they see them far too often. That's the secret of successful strategy — make use of the ordinary. It happens all the time so nobody notices. Nobody really sees what they're accustomed to seeing. And little dogs like to linger at telephone boxes. So watch your chance and that's it — you're through! And there aren't so many low bushes on that side, easier terrain altogether."

"I see."

"Reserved strictly for the use of personnel on duty, of course," Shaky warned, and Matt agreed, "Of course."

"Things can't go on like this," Shaky said mournfully. "One doesn't want to go about spreading alarm and despondency among civilians, but the Bishop will have to take decisive action. And the ranks are thinning, there aren't so many of us left now. The Misses Tomlinson are gone and the Reverend Mr. Robinson and my own benefactor, Mrs. L'Estrange." At the mention of this lady's name the two little dogs stood up on their hind legs solemnly and then sat down. "Showing their esteem and gratitude," Shaky explained. "As I was saying, there's not many of us left. There's Theodore Taffe, of course, you'd think he'd care. But his heart was never really in it — half the time he used to be late for Choir practices, and then on Sundays he'd make every hymn a personal appearance, with his mind on his profile instead of his Maker. Not like young Queenie Harrison. Ah, there was a voice! When she sang 'I know that My Redeemer liveth' — she knew, all right. Poor Queenie's had a sad time, I hear. And there's no one else."

Matt glanced over at Eddie, and though it was too dark to be sure he thought he saw in his eyes the support he was asking for. He leaned forward. "There's us now, Mr. Frick," he said.

Shaky stared. "What do you mean, boy? Who are 'us'?"

So Matt took a breath and told him about the gang and how they had found their way to the inside of the Square and to the church, and what they had discovered there, and what they had learned from Miss Harrison ("Young Queenie Harrison") about the history of St. George's.

"Ha! Reinforcements! That's the stuff," Shaky declared. "The Bishop will hear about this in my next dispatch. This will be a boost to our morale. I was aware, of course, that some unauthorized person or persons had been around this week. And there's a strange cat that thinks he's billeted on St. George — the little dogs don't care for him!"

"He's all right," Matt said. "He's called the Dragon, and he's One of Us, too." He looked at Eddie again, and this time he was sure that Eddie nodded. "Other people have been around as well as us." And he told about the chaps on the roof and how they'd cleared off because of Gwen, and that they'd come back earlier in the evening, and what he had overheard them saying.

Shaky was delighted. "Aha! Things begin to move. General Alert and Action Stations!"

"What is it they're after anyway?" Matt inquired. "I mean, what is there on the roof?"

"Don't you know? Don't you really know?" Shaky asked and turned from Matt to Eddie. And in that instant Matt realized for sure that Eddie did know, had known all along, and was amused at Matt's innocence.

"Lead, boy, lead," Shaky said. "That's the loot! Beautiful lead, up on the roof, lying around waiting for anybody with a pair of snippers to strip it. Valuable stuff, lead is. Plenty of ways of getting rid of it, big money and no questions asked. And St. George left open to the wind and rain. Just another ruin. And the local brass hats will only remember about it when it becomes dangerous, and one morning the people who live in the houses round about will wake up and hear demolition squads and bulldozers and the whine of the saws as the trees come down, and they'll discover that there was an inside to the railings as well as an outside. And they'll wonder why nobody ever told them."

"Why don't we tell them?"

"No use, boy. It's machinery that people listen to nowadays, not voices."

The dogs had grown impatient and Shaky said it was time he took them back to the billet. But he would write a special dispatch to the Bishop, he repeated. Meantime additional patrols exercising initiative and discretion would be welcome. Communication outside the railings was strictly forbidden for security reasons, except in a top-level emergency. "Their spies are everywhere!" he said. Reports of new enemy activity could be exchanged inside, nightly, at nine-thirty pip emma. Care must be taken at all times, cunning must be set against cunning. Finally he declared, "These are dangerous and desperate men," and then, "tootle-oo!" and he and the little dogs were gone so quickly that not even a movement from a branch betrayed their route.

"He's as loony as they come," Eddie commented, "plain bats, but everything he says is true."

"Then you did go up on the roof with the Flint kids to have a look because that chap asked you to."

"Told me," Eddie corrected, "that bloke doesn't ask. The kids hadn't a clue what it was all about, they thought it was a game."

"And you passed it on to Dan-boy that the lead was there, waiting for him."

"If I did," snarled Eddie, "why do you think he had to come and look for himself? I've been dodging him for a week."

Matt didn't answer, just pulled grass and chewed it. Eddie said, "You have to believe something I say some time." Matt spat out the grass which was rough and hairy and rolled around on his elbows. "What's it like up there, anyway?" he asked, and Eddie said it wasn't bad and why not come and take a look, and Matt said he didn't mind if he did but they hadn't got Ma Flint's stepladder, and Eddie said he'd only brought it for the Flint kids, it was easy without it.

So Matt said, "What are we waiting for, then?" and he followed Eddie, onto a window ledge, up a drainpipe, then by a precarious balance on a parapet and a long arm extended to the crest of the roof, and up and over, and he and Eddie were sitting astride the summit.

"Lead," Eddie said, stroking the surface below his knees as he rode it like a horse, "all lovely, lovely lead."

"It'd be easy. Anybody could do it. Like taking the skin off a banana!"

"And acres more of it up on the roof of the church. Like to come?"

Fingers, elbows and knees pressed against the right angle of the wall and a buttress, then a strong haul around a convenient pinnacle with ground, stone wall and sky momentarily wheeling dizzily, and they had made it, had reached the flatly tilted expanse on the church's roof. It was like the deck of a ship, riding in a sea of plunging branches.

"They said they would need a 'double-twenty' before they could take the lead from up here," Matt said. "That was what it sounded like. do you know what a double-twenty is?"

Eddie shook his head. They made a brief inspection of their territory and settled to inspect the view.

"Gosh! I like it up here!" Matt said.

The tower, rising above them startlingly near and solid, was a gentle gold color. The weathercock on his perch, so close that Matt could see its separate feathers, was gold too. Eddie's face looked gold, like the face of a gilded statue. There was a commotion in the trees at their eye level, and the owl rose untidily, to discover what sort of a night it was. He sank out of sight again and they heard him voicing his approval. "He does it the proper way," Eddie said and laughed, and Matt laughed too, feeling at ease with Eddie for the first time he could remember.

Around the edges of the Square the lights in the street and in the houses appeared dull and insignificant. The moon was the true source of all light. The people in the houses had shut it out with colored curtains and had forgotten about it and were busy living matchbox lives in their own patterns.

"Can't we do something to surprise them?" Matt suggested. "Something to make them push the curtains back and open their windows and look out and take some notice? I'd like to shout and yell and do a war dance and ring bells and fly flags and wake them all up. They always do the same things Sunday evenings. Mum will be watching the telly now, the hymn-singing, and complaining about the ladies' hats — either they aren't wearing any or they're looking frights. What'll your mum be doing, Eddie?"

Eddie said, "Out," and Matt was sorry he'd asked. But

he thought of Mr. Ricardo presiding over the acres of golden chips, and Mr. Lumba stretched half asleep on the sofa dandling the nearest baby and singing to it very soft and low, a lion's growl of a song, and Cousin Maudie painting her nails green, and Gwen's big sister reading glossies, and Ma Flint eating chocolates and scolding anyone who was near enough to scold. And Dan-boy — wherever he and his associates might be — plotting his dark plots and scheming what he could do with a double-twenty.

"I suppose we could tell the Police," he said to Eddie.

Eddie just said, "We couldn't, not on your life," and finished that idea.

"We'll beat them ourselves then," Matt declared, "that's what we'll do!"

"Us kids and old Shaky Frick?" Eddie sounded scornful. "Those chaps aren't playing games, you know." Then he said, "But we will, too."

There was a scrambling scrapy sound close at hand, and the head of the Dragon appeared above the parapet. It hesitated, widening its yellow eyes as if it was scandalized at the idea of boys who had taken to life on the rooftops. Then it completed the hoist over the top, and came stepping on precise paws to join them.

In a small stir of wind the weathercock shuddered and swung creakily, and settled back in its place again. The owl, thoroughly awake, left his branch with economical skill and set off on the night's business. Matt stretched his hand out to the Dragon, and saw with approval that its whiskers were golden too.

6

GWEN always enjoyed being shocked by the wickedness of other people, and when Madge told her on the way to school next morning what Matt had discovered about Dan-boy and his friends — Madge had been told by Sidney who had heard it firsthand from Matt — she "Oohed!" and "Aahed!" righteously with eyes like saucers; and after Assembly when the Headmaster announced that because of the measles epidemic in the neighborhood all schools were to be closed for a fortnight and so they could go home, she declared at once that this was an Act of God, although of course it was an act of the City's Chief Medical Officer. But whoever was responsible, it was certainly most convenient.

Almost every child in Dove Square had had measles at the earliest opportunity, some of them twice, so it was really more in the nature of a holiday, a holiday that they could put to a good purpose. And after they had come back and told any parents who were around what the Headmaster had said (Madge's weird Cousin Maudie who was giving herself a tawny-chestnut rinse raised her eyes to Heaven and said, "Give me patience" and put her head back into the basin) they congregated on the steps for a brief parley. This was briefer than they intended because Ma Flint appeared in the porch with a mop and a bucket of soapy water and told them that if they hadn't any work to do they could at least get out from under the feet of the people who had, and already the blue-gray suds were halfway down the steps, chasing them.

They had drifted onto the square of grass in front, and were settling to business when Cousin Maudie's head appeared at a window — tawny-chestnut rivers running like snakes down her brow — and she threw out half a crown and told Madge to get cod fillet for dinner and to tell Mr. Taffe that she knew what a cod fillet looked like as well as he did. So realizing that they were too near their homes for any real peace (poor Madge collected the half crown with the look of one who accepts a tragic fate) they moved out onto the pavement.

This was no good either because there was a squad of men replacing broken pavings. "Go and get lost, there's good kids," one of them said. They shifted a little further up the Square, envying birds who have such a lavish choice of trees and branches and secret hiding places, and ants who are small enough to make use of the space under a stone.

"Where'll we go?"

"The tunnel?"

"No," Matt said. He was growing accustomed to hearing his own voice by this time, it no longer took him by surprise and people seemed to have forgotten to call him Doormatt. "The chaps might be there."

"Not in the morning; they'll be out at work."

"D'you think Dan-boy works?" Eddie said scaldingly. "And Matt's right, they've guessed we were fooling them. If we had the keys to show, it would be all right, but we haven't. And next time they catch us over there they won't believe us."

"Where, then?"

They looked at Matt. Rain had begun to fall on the pavement in soft lazy spots that promised more. There must be an empty space somewhere that was under cover. Somewhere that didn't cost money. Somewhere where there was a reason for them to be and where they were allowed to talk. Somewhere Dan-boy wouldn't happen to see them. The Launderette might have done, but being Monday it would be fuller than usual of Mums and prams and babies.

"Where, Matt?"

"The Museum," Matt decided. "It's the best. Meet you where the tanks of fish are. Better not go in a gang, either. Everyone find their own way."

So at the end of half an hour they had packed by twos and threes into the Aquarium of the City Museum, where it was warm and quiet, and only a ten-spined Stickleback or a Gudgeon (*Gobio gobio,* the label said) circling in their rectangles of golden water could watch them or had a chance to overhear what was said, and they didn't seem interested in anything except their own sudden sorties into the weeds and out again.

Then Matt, with Eddie's assistance, told the gang everything that had happened, about the men and their conversation, about Shaky Frick and his patrols and his correspondence with the Bishop, about Henry's clue of the cigarette packet, about Gwen's big sister's boy friend, about the lead on the roof and what would happen to St. George's when it was peeled off. The younger kids who hadn't heard it earlier gasped and grew solemn and Sidney said, "Most large villains," which summed up what everybody was feeling.

They had begun to discuss a plan of action, perhaps a little energetically, when a man in a stiff peaked cap put his head in and gave them a curious look and after a minute he came back and asked if they were interested in the fish and Henry said thank you very much yes they were, and the man said that probably other people might be interested as well and that they'd better be moving along to give them the chance, and Henry said they were just waiting for the Perch (family Percidae), distinguished by a large spring fin on its back which can be raised and lowered at will, to decide whether he was going to raise or lower it, and the man said was that so and went away, but not very far. So they knew they'd have to shift and they climbed to the gallery higher up where there were boxes of gold coins that had recently been excavated in the neighborhood. But these turned out to be much more interesting than the fish had been and people began to forget what they had come for and to feel the urge to rush off into the wide open spaces and start digging right away, and in any case the man in the stiff peaked cap had come to the foot of the stairs and was leaning on the banister rail watching them, and a

statue at the end of the gallery had got his eye on them as well, so they had to move once more. "Like the Children of Israel," Gwen said.

They found refuge at last in a quiet corner on the top

story among glass cases with lumps of rock in them (yellow ochre whose yellow color was due to the ochre derived from once over-lying Triassic rocks). This stirred nobody's imagination, so they were able to settle down to business.

"We've got to find out all we can about these chaps, that's the first thing." And Eddie said he knew as much as he wanted about them, thank *you* very much, and Matt said well what did they know, he'd never seen them, he'd only heard them talking, and Gwen said she'd been too busy singing to have a real look, and Madge said that was a fat lot of use, did she have to sing with her eyes closed, and then Matt remembered that of course he had seen Dan-boy and so had Eddie.

"Well then — what's he like?"

Dan-boy had been just ordinary, that was the trouble. He hadn't a wooden leg or a scar on his cheek or a squint; apart from the particularly unpleasant look of pleasure on his face while he was twisting Eddie's arm at the corner of the Square that evening, Matt couldn't remember anything distinctive about him. Eddie, when they appealed to him, said, "Just like anybody else, I suppose," in a tone of deep loathing that implied there wasn't much difference between one snake and the next.

Then, suddenly, somebody remembered Gwen's big sister.

"Of course! She can help!"

Gwen said she couldn't, not any more, and Eddie said, "She goes around with him, doesn't she?" and Gwen said not now she didn't, not after he'd stood her up on Friday evening. "It's Rupert she goes with now," she explained. Matt said that was quick work, and Gwen said, "She always goes off and on very quick," and Matt said "Women!" and Gwen said it was better than stealing the lead off churches and anyway her big sister's Stars last week had said she would have a change in her romantic life, and Eddie said it was a pity she couldn't have hung on a week longer, and Gwen said you couldn't go against the Stars, and Eddie asked why couldn't you, and Gwen tightened her sharp nose and said you couldn't expect boys to understand things like that.

"Maybe he gave her a photograph," someone suggested, "and she forgot to give it back. You could have a look, Gwen, couldn't you?" and Gwen said her sister would kill her and someone said in that case Gwen would be a martyr and Gwen said it wasn't a thing to make jokes about and whoever it was said they weren't joking.

They decided in the end that it would be wisest for the gang to patrol in couples inside the railings, and report to Matt when the next couple had taken over duty from them. Two children with their wits about them could keep out of the enemy's way, melting into grass and bushes before they had been spotted. They might go inside the church if they wanted to, by way of the window, but if they did this they must be particularly careful that they weren't being watched. They were to avoid the times when Corporal Frick and his detachment were on patrol unless there was something of particular importance that needed to be passed on to him ("No use duplicating personnel" Eddie said to Matt in a Shaky Frick voice). If anybody saw anything that looked like a "double-twenty" lying around Matt was to be told at once, as this could mean that action might be imminent. And if Gwen could produce a photograph of Dan-boy or winkle any information about him out of her sister that would be grand. Sidney, who took pride in doing such things and had a large battery of colored pens, was to make out a patrol rota with names and times, and they were all to be given a copy.

And so the meeting broke up, and they left the Museum feeling that a good morning's work had been done.

Unexpected sunshine was bleaching the wet pavements. Madge was the last to step into it, but in her present mood she didn't notice that it had rained or had stopped raining. Cousin Maudie's half crown tied in a hankie in the pocket of her cardigan had spoiled the morning's excitement for her. She had been careful to dodge Gwen because she knew Gwen was eager to go into a feminine huddle with her about life in general and boys in particular, and so she didn't leave the building until she was sure everyone else had cleared off. But halfway through the revolving glass door she realized that she had left too soon. The Trailer had become unhitched from Henry and was sitting on the top of the steps looking miserable, not knowing how to get back to Dove Square on his own.

Madge felt a sharp tug of impatience. Not again! Henry'd been doing this too often. She didn't want to be stuck with the kid. But he seemed so dreary and brightened so quickly when he spotted her that she said, "Oh all right. I suppose you'll have to come with me then," and was aware of a double shadow as she turned into the street and of a second set of footsteps, lighter and quicker than her own.

"I've got to fetch fish on the way," she threw at him over her shoulder, hoping this might discourage him, but the Trailer nodded and smiled and said, "Fish and chips! Fish and chips!" as if it was a splendid idea, and there was no use explaining.

She wished that she was in Gwen's shoes. How thoroughly and with what pleasure she would have gone through Gwen's big sister's private belongings — every now and again she did it with Cousin Maudie's — and if, between a Slim-Quick Sheet torn from a magazine and a free sample of face cream, she found a photograph of Dan-boy, what praise and credit she would win from the gang. She wasn't going to get any credit from Cousin Maudie when she arrived back with the cod fillet, but she had an idea what she'd get if she came back without it.

She tried not to think of the smiling Mr. Taffe, Select Fishmonger and Poulterer, presiding behind his slabs of dead fish and below the curtains of dead swinging birds. In any case, what he really looked like when you saw him was always much more frightening than anything you had been able to imagine beforehand. She tried not to think of the veiled eyes of the upside-down birds and the fishes' mouths still open after they had expelled the final suffocating gasp. It was Cousin Maudie who had told her about Mr. Taffe's mesmeric powers, and half the things Cousin Maudie said were clean crackers, anyway. And yet she knew that when she made her request for cod fillet to the middle button of Mr. Taffe's white coat and then felt her eyes pulled up to his face, as they would be, she would need all her courage. Cod fillet, please, Mr. Taffe, half a crown's worth, and Cousin Maudie says you know the way she likes it. Oh those eyes that seemed to widen into oceans and draw her towards them. And though she didn't believe that one day she would totter back to Cousin Maudie wreathed around with salmon, like Mrs. Ellis from the corner (with half a crown there wasn't much chance) she was afraid the day would come when all her will power would be sucked into those oceans and she would be stretched out, senseless on a slab, among the fish.

She thought it might help her to think about the photograph that Miss Harrison had shown them of the Sunday School outing with a small Theodore Taffe looking a bit of a drip in his sailor suit ("A very tiresome little boy, I'm afraid") but the sulky child had no connection with the white-coated smiling man.

You smelled the fish shop before you reached it. This was when the terror first started to creep, and Madge's step slowed. The Trailer caught up with her, the kid still grinning in an aggravating way. "Well, come on then if you're coming," she snapped and grabbed his hand, giving it a bad-tempered jerk so that he wouldn't guess she was doing it for her own comfort. The air of the fish shop now reached them, salt and strong. Madge took a deep breath and dived into the shadow of the striped awning.

It was empty except for Mr. Taffe and his fish. She knew he was there without needing to look, and kept her eyes on her feet as she crossed the tiled floor to the counter.

"Well well, Redhead," said the dread voice, "and to what do we owe the pleasure of your company this bright and dewy morning?"

"Half a crown's worth of cod fillet, please, Mr. Taffe, and Cousin Maudie says — "

"We'll skip Cousin Maudie this morning, shall we? Here we are then, cod fillet so fresh that there's still a wiggle left in its tail!"

His hands, which were long and large, reached out and lifted something from the slab with a kind of careless love. One hand took a knife and held it, estimating how much half a crown would buy.

"Left school and become a lady, have you, Redhead?" Mr. Taffe asked. The question had a kind of a threat in it. Cousin Maudie was fond of saying things like this. And now Mr. Taffe was bending across the counter towards her and the moment had come. She looked up at him and began to explain about the school being off because of the measles epidemic, trying to keep her mind on the ridged half crown which was now pressed tightly between her palms. His eyes today were like the cods' eyes on the slab. Her knees had become soft as licorice. And then someone came into the shop and stood beside her, a large man with his hands in his pockets who was saying, "Hallo there, Theo, you old shark!" She felt dizzy with relief.

"And hallo and good morning to you," Mr. Taffe replied. He cut the fish expertly, wrapped it in a parcel with a single movement of his wrists and slapped it into Madge's hands. "Cod fillet as per specification from Cousin Maudie," he said, "ta very much, Redhead," and he took the half crown.

It was her dismissal and release. It was all over and she had survived. She was turning for the door and had heard the ring of the till as Mr. Taffe put the money into it, had almost won her way into the street, when Mr. Taffe spoke again, this time to his other customer.

I didn't hear it, he didn't say it, that wasn't what he called him, she told herself, and took two more steps towards liberty — and stopped, plundering her imagination for any excuse she could scrape up for staying here a little longer. Dan-boy! She had heard. She must stay. She couldn't slink off now.

The occasion demanded heroism, there was no wriggling out.

"Forgotten something, gorgeous?" Mr. Taffe called after her.

She felt dizzy and mumbled, "No." The dizziness persisted and with it inspiration came. Of course! Why not feel dizzy? Dizzier and dizzier.

"Bang-bang, we're dead!" she said softly to the Trailer,

and collapsed on the floor of the shop as she had always
imagined she might do, though with much more pleasure than she had thought possible. Even before she hit
the floor she thought what a performance she was giving.
The Trailer wasn't doing badly, either. He had taken
the cue without a murmur and was stretched beside

her, out for the count, in a game that was familiar, though he'd never played it on a fish shop's floor.

She kept her eyes tightly closed and awaited developments with interest. Even when her hand was lifted and held between two large hands she remained as limp as the cod fillet in its parcel.

"Passed out, the pair of them! Well, what do you know?" It was Mr. Taffe's voice. "Sickening for the measles or something, I thought she looked a bit peaky," and the man said, "What do we do now?" and Mr. Taffe said, "Better bring them into the back for a sit-down — can't have the place looking like a Casualty Station, bad for business." Then she was carried through a door and set down in a chair, where she allowed her head to loll convincingly.

"Here!" Mr. Taffe's voice again. "Try a drink of this." The hard rim of a cup was set against her mouth. She opened her eyes for a brief unseeing moment, the way people did it on the telly, and fluttered her lids and lowered them again.

"Real bad," Mr. Taffe said. "Maybe we'd better send for her Cousin Maudie," so she fluttered her eyes open again, and said, "Oh, Mr. Taffe!," smiling, as if he'd been Father Christmas.

"How are you feeling, kid? Better now?"

She said she'd be all right in a minute, but could she just sit still where she was. "Sure, sure!" Mr. Taffe said. "Take it easy and Uncle Theo'll come back in a minute. O.K.?" so she nodded weakly, wishing that Gwen

118

and the boys could see, and Mr. Taffe and Dan-boy went back into the shop.

As soon as they had gone the Trailer who was draped in another chair, bobbed up excitedly, ready for the next move.

"Hush! You're still dead!" Madge snapped, and he passed out obediently once more.

The little room at the back was surprisingly snug and ordinary, not at all what she had expected. Fancy Mr. Taffe having an armchair and a gas ring and a colored calendar on the wall, just like any ordinary person. Together with the elation she felt in her achievement came the glorious certainty that never again would a journey to the fish shop be an occasion of terror.

Out in the shop the men were talking. The door was partially open. Dan-boy told Mr. Taffe that he'd looked round on Saturday week but the shop was closed.

"Funeral," Mr. Taffe said, "old Harrison, from Dove Square. What was it brought you this way?"

"A friendly call."

"Which means — ?" asked Mr. Taffe, and Dan-boy laughed and said he had a suspicious mind, and he'd take a couple of pairs of kippers while he was there, and who was Harrison, anyway, the name rang a bell.

"So did he," said Mr. Taffe, "plenty of them. He used to be the sexton at St. George Without. Yours truly sang in the choir with him."

"Did you now? I heard somewhere that you had quite a voice, Theo my old shark."

"Oh I don't know about that," Mr. Taffe said in the

kind of voice that meant he did. "Two pairs of kippers, was it?"

"Make it three."

Mr. Taffe made it three.

"So he looked after the church did he?" Dan-boy said. "Pity about the old place. No word of them opening it up again, I suppose?"

"Time and again you hear rumors but nothing definite. Miss Harrison was in this morning, she'd have mentioned it if there'd been anything. She'd be the one to know."

"The old man's daughter?"

"That's right. She was in the Choir too, real peach of a voice. She used to give the kids piano lessons before they all had transistors or got themselves a guitar on the H.P. Dressmaking she does now."

The kippers had been wrapped and paid for.

"Well, I'll push off."

"Sure there's nothing else you want along with the kippers?"

Dan-boy laughed and said something that Madge couldn't hear. The outside door opened for a moment to admit street noises. Dan-boy had gone.

Mr. Taffe was pleased to find his two invalids considerably recovered when he came back into the little room again. "No hurry," he told them, "don't try to move until you're sure you're all right." Madge said she was sure, thank you very much, and as she went through the shop she took enormous pleasure in tottering for a moment and putting her hand down on the cold counter which had now no terror for her at all. "Quite all right, thank you, Mr. Taffe," she said, and if her voice trembled she was pleased to think how excellently it fitted the part. "And thank you very much for everything."

"Say no more. I don't have beautiful redheads swooning in my shop every day in the week." He opened the door for them, and if instead of closing it and returning to his counter he had followed them out for a moment into the street, he would have been puzzled to see his pair of casualties skipping down the pavement like spring lambs, Madge brandishing the parcel of cod fillet while her red plaits bumped on her shoulders, and the Trailer traveling alternately by cartwheels and somersaults.

There was no sign of Matt when they got back to Dove Square. Henry, sitting halfway up the steps with his mouth plugged with toffee and his eyes hooked into a comic, told Madge that Eddie and Matt were on duty up the tunnel.

"What's up, anyway?" he inquired. "You're looking pleased with yourself." Madge said she had an important report to make to Matt and Henry said come on, tell him, couldn't she, and she said it had to be Matt. So he said, "Bet you it isn't all that important," and went back to sucking and reading, and the Trailer lay down quietly at the other side of the comic to get a view of the pictures, and Henry said, "Where did you get to, anyway?" without looking up.

Madge sprawled on the bed in the room she shared

with Cousin Maudie and allowed the full tide of success to flow through her. How brave and how clever she had been! What a report she had to make! Wait till the boys heard about this. She knew where Cousin Maudie hid her special scented notepaper and helped herself to a page of it on which to write down a detailed description of Dan-boy.

Dan-boy. Well, now. Begin at the beginning. Dan-boy was tall. Oh yes, definitely tall. What else? Well, he was tall, like I said. Young or old? Well, not what you'd call old. I mean not really *old,* well, I suppose he was young, then. And his face? What did he look like? Oh yes — his face. This was difficult. First of all he'd been standing beside her, more behind her, really, and later on she'd had her eyes closed most of the time—well, your eyes would be closed if you'd gone flat out in a swoon. Anyway there wasn't anything really special about his face. His hair, then — fair or dark? Well, neither, really, when you came to think about it. It was long, of course. What else? Wait a minute. Brown shoes! She was almost sure he'd been wearing brown shoes with very long points; yes, she was sure she remembered them quite close to her flatties on the white tiles of Mr. Taffe's floor. Yes, but afterwards, when you sat up and said you were feeling better, so that they wouldn't send for Cousin Maudie, you had your eyes open then, hadn't you? Slowly, coldly, the lovely sense of achievement seeped out of her. She was no better than Gwen. She could imagine Henry — "Next time you pass out in a fish shop do it with your eyes open, will you?" And Eddie — "Girls!" And Matt.

Cousin Maudie said at dinnertime that when she went to the trouble to cook cod fillet it was a pity people hadn't enough civility to eat it and what was the matter with her, anyway? And Madge took a long time to wash up afterwards. She tried closing her eyes again to see if Dan-boy's face would appear before her but it didn't and the washing-up water got cold and greasy. While she was finishing, Cousin Maudie, dressed in her best and with her hair shouting out loud, announced that she was off to the Pictures. After she had gone a soft clod of soil hit the kitchen window and Madge knew that the boys were there, waiting for her and her important report. So she dried her hands as slowly as she could and went out.

There they were, Matt, Sidney, Henry and Eddie, all goggling, with Gwen on the edge.

"Come on," they commanded, "tell!"

"The rest of you go away," Madge said. "I want to talk to Matt by himself." Matt said, "Hop it," and the others went a few yards up the street, crossly and slowly. "Now, get on with it," Matt said.

He squatted on the steps with her and she told. She told about her excursion to the fish shop and how the stranger had come in, and how by her extreme quickness of wit she had noticed Mr. Taffe calling him "Dan-boy." "Go on," Matt said. She told him of her wonderfully inspired swoon on the fish shop floor, of her slow and dramatic recovery, of the open door, of her cunning eavesdropping and of the men's conversation. Matt's ears were flapping. "Go on!"

"And after that he went away," she said.

"Yes, but what did he look like?"

She closed her eyes for a last chance of a miracle, but it was no use, no face appeared in the darkness inside her lids. "Come on — what did he *look* like?" Matt insisted. And she opened her eyes.

Down the steps towards her a pair of brown shoes with very long points were approaching. In a moment of blissful recognition she gripped Matt's arm and held it. He yelped and she gripped tighter and he got the message and shut up. The shoes went past, had turned up the pavement, were almost at the zebra crossing. She released Matt's arm.

He rubbed it and asked, "What was that in aid of?"

"That was him!"

"That was who?"

"That man — it was Dan-boy!"

"Where?"

Dan-boy was on the other side of the street, was disappearing into a shop.

"So it is!" Matt said. "Where did he come from?"

"From Miss Harrison's door," Madge said, "he came out from there."

"If Eddie and I hadn't been up the tunnel," Matt said, "we'd have spotted him going in."

He whistled the others and told them. "Watch that shop. Anybody that comes out, trail them."

"Not me," Eddie said. "I saw who came out just now. That's as near as I want to get."

"Henry and Sidney then. Eddie stay here and give them a sign when he leaves the shop. Madge come with me."

They mounted the steps and knocked on Miss Harrison's door. She opened it. They found they hadn't any words ready. Then Matt invented words.

"That man who was here — the man who just went away. He wasn't looking for my Mum, was he? The man about the Insurance was to come today, and I was to look out for him and give him the money."

"No, no," Miss Harrison said, brisk and smiling, "that was the piano tuner. Such an agreeable young man. He tells me he's trying to work up a business for himself in the neighborhood. I was so sorry I couldn't make use of him but a piano tuner is rather a luxury for me, you know. However, I made him a cup of tea and we talked and he seemed to go off quite satisfied."

Matt's eyes traveled to the hook beside the fireplace. It was empty.

"I'll bet he did," Matt said.

7

HENRY and Sidney who had been keeping watch outside the shop made signs from the other side of the road that the man had not yet appeared. Matt beckoned them home for a quick conference, sending two of the junior Flints to take over the watch. He told them briefly that Dan-boy had visited Miss Harrison to ask if he could tune her piano and that when he had gone the keys of St. George Without had gone with him. "He went in while we were up the tunnel and he was there all the time we were eating our dinner." Their dinner lay heavily in their guilty stomachs. "If you'd told us before dinner, Madge, we might have guessed he'd try Miss Harrison."

"You were up the tunnel before dinner," Madge snapped.

"Well, what do we do now?"

"We've got to get those keys back, that's what. While they've got the keys we can't go near the place. They're certain now that we were fooling them. Unless we can get the keys back it's all washed up."

Henry said, "There's always the Police," but one look at Eddie finished that idea.

"We've got to trail him," Matt said, "find out where he goes, where he lives — "

"Who'll do it?"

"Not Gwen. Not Madge. Not Eddie."

"Scared, are you?" Henry said sideways to Eddie, but before Eddie had a chance to answer, Matt said, "You are a nit, Henry. Dan-boy knows what Gwen and Madge and Eddie look like. They can't go. I've seen him but he hasn't seen me. So it'll be me and you and Sidney. Three's enough. He won't notice us."

"He might just notice Sidney," someone said.

No one looked at Sidney's black face and Sidney didn't say anything but Matt knew that he was watching him and that it was for him to decide. The Doormatt days had had their advantages.

"Sidney's coming," he said, "and the girls and the Trailer can take over from whoever's turn it was at St. George Without until we're back. And Eddie and the Flints can be on duty here, in case anything happens that matters."

"That's going to be lively for us, isn't it?" Eddie grumbled. "I hope the excitement won't be too much for me."

Matt said, "It would be crazy if you came," and Eddie said, "I didn't say I wanted to, did I?" and Henry said, "I knew you were scared," and anything might have happened after that if it hadn't been for a cunning needle of a whistle from one of the Flints, at least it must have come from them, but those kids knew their business and were apparently engaged in a wrestling

match outside the shop across the road, from whose door
Dan-boy had just emerged.

"Come on, you two," Matt snapped, and Henry and
Sidney followed him across the street.

If you are walking along a street for some common or

CITY BATHS

SWIM
AND

Keep fit

MIXED
BATHING
DAILY

garden purpose with somewhere to go, such as coming back from school or on a message or something, you don't think about it. It is quite ordinary. You just walk and stop for a bit if you feel like it and mooch and stare into a shop window and laugh if there's anything funny to laugh at and try the cigarette machines in case there's any money left in them, although there isn't, and go on again. You don't think of the people who see you doing it. But when you are trailing a villain, keeping him in sight but pretending you aren't even interested in what he does with himself, finding a reason to stop when he stops and for going on again when he goes on and making it all look as if you'd meant to do it yourself anyway, you feel as if you have walked out of a fancy dress party into the street and that everybody has noticed and even the dogs and the lampposts are watching you. Your feet grow inches on them, and if you try to whistle no sound comes, and when you hang around as if you were waiting for the ice cream van, people stare and you know for sure that they know that this isn't the time the ice cream van comes this way. Henry, Matt thought, looked as guilty as if he'd been robbing a bank, and that was the way he was feeling too. Only Sidney, scuffing a lemonade top between his feet, looked ordinary. He was glad he had decided that Sidney could come.

Dan-boy, after he had left the shop, spent some time examining the watches in the jeweler's at the corner. He read the posters outside the cinema and looked at the pictures in the frames. He said, "Hiya!" to a pair of pretty girls who put up their noses like duchesses and giggled when they'd got past. He collected a parcel from the Quick Cleaners. And in and out of doorways, feeling like criminals who expect a heavy hand on their shoulder at any moment, Matt and Henry mooned and dodged and chased, envying Sidney the easy little tune he was occupied with, and his black impassive face.

Once they were held up when the light changed at the street crossing and Dan-boy was over ahead of them, but it was a relief when the next green light released them to go weaving and bumping along through the crowds on the pavement until they had almost caught up with him again.

He had stopped at a shop where a notice was pasted in the window that read "Opening Shortly." Inside the shop carpenters were working at the half-completed counters and shelves. The boys, advancing too enthusiastically, overshot the shop, passing Dan-boy at its entrance, where he had paused to light a cigarette. They smelled the tobacco mixed with the sharp smell of the raw wood. Then Matt invented a stone in his shoe and they halted and waited while he took the shoe off and shook it. This took some time. One of the carpenters had come to the shop's door and was talking to Dan-boy; something was arranged between them. Matt caught the tone of the man's voice though not the words and remembered hearing it outside the window of the committee room. "That's one of them," he said to Henry. Henry in his excitement turned a bright flaring pink, like instant scarlet fever, and looked away. Only Sidney, whistling breathily between his teeth, found it possible to stare. "I fix that face in my brain same as glue," he said. Dan-boy left his friend and was moving on.

They had come as far as the Public Baths now, but

none of them foresaw that Dan-boy would cross the road suddenly and go inside.

"Look at that!"

"He can't just go for a swim!"

"That's what he has done."

"What to do now, please?" asked Sidney, picking up the lemonade top and putting it in his pocket.

Henry's face suddenly appeared to be inspired, like a light coming on from inside. "If he's gone for a swim then he's going to take off his clothes."

"People do," Matt said. He was getting a bit fed up with Henry.

"Yes, but you absolute birdbrain, and loon, you idiot, don't you see — ?"

And then Matt saw.

He saw the possibilities and recognized that they were impossible in one lightning moment. The keys of St. George Without were lying in a pocket of the clothes that Dan-boy was about to take off. Anyone who knew they were there could — might — but they had no money, no tickets to admit them into the Baths, no hope at all. Dan-boy would have his swim and come out again and reclaim his clothes and the keys would still be in his pocket. Unless — he looked at Henry. Saturday evening choir practice at the Cathedral was the time he got his money. He couldn't have chewed his way all through it so early in the week. Matt didn't have to say anything. Henry knew what he was thinking. Heroically he said, "Oh. All right then," and put his hand into his pocket.

"Three," he said to the man at the turnstile.

"And suits and towels," prompted Matt.

Henry gulped and put down more money. "And suits and towels." The man issued the tickets and they went in.

Dan-boy was already in the water by the time they had stripped and put their clothes in the wire cages and taken them along to the attendant and collected the discs with the numbers on them to wear on their wrists. They fooled around at the shallow end, putting their toes in and taking them out, squealing like kids and plotting under their breath. Dan-boy was ploughing up and down the Baths in a powerful crawl, touching the bar at each end and turning, like a mahogany-colored sea lion. There were only a few other swimmers in the water, none of them expert. Dan-boy approached the shallow end for the third time.

"Now," said Matt, and barged into Sidney, and Sidney fell into the water just where you thought Dan-boy's powerful carcass would carve him in half. But Sidney had slid sideways like a fish and was surfacing just as Dan-boy's hand shot out to grasp the rail for the turn. It was his right hand.

"Did you get it?" Matt whispered as they hauled Sidney over the side, and he shook the water out of his ears and said, "It was thirty-three."

Dan-boy had reached the deep end again and had climbed out and was chatting to the attendant. They seemed to have a lot to say to each other. "All in together!" Matt yelled, pulling the other two with him, and they fell noisily backwards into the water and struggled to the rail and jumped up and down like an Infants' Class, making their final plans between laughter and mouthfuls of water. "And there's something more," Matt gasped, "he didn't come here for a swim, he came to talk to that attendant. There's another face for you to glue, Sidney."

After that everything went swimmingly, as Matt told the rest of the gang afterwards, and they forgave him the joke because it was so absolutely right, the only thing that Matt could have said.

Sidney padded to the deep end and climbed the ladder to the very highest diving board and went out to the extreme edge of it and stood there, bouncing a little, swinging his arms and raising his chin, looking as if he was going off it and then deciding not to at the last minute. Everyone always watches anyone at the end of the high diving board and they watched Sidney. From the shallow end Matt and Henry gave him mock applause, and Sidney bowed and almost overbalanced but just didn't, and everyone said, "Oooh!" and then Sidney curled his toes round the edge of the board and stood up very straight and serious, which meant that this was really it.

"You up there! Sure you know what you're doing, kid?" the attendant called. And Sidney — how well he did it! — looked startled and one leg went up and this time he really did overbalance and came through the air with arms and legs sticking out in all directions. He reached the water with a tremendous wallop, throwing up showers of spray, and bobbed to the surface and waved his arms about wildly and went down again, and was just about to go down for the third time when Matt came in on his cue and shouted, "Help! Help!" and jumped in at the shallow end to swim to Sidney, and had gone about a third of the length of the Baths when he threw his arms up and sank, guggling. "Help! Help!" yelled Henry in turn, jumping up and down at the shallow end.

Then things really got moving. Dan-boy dived into the water to fish for Sidney but somehow or other Sidney didn't happen to be there when he arrived, or maybe he was slippery or something, and the attendant ran for his long pole with the hook on it, and he poked it at Matt and Matt snatched at it but missed and went down again, and the attendant yelled for the man who looked after the wire cages full of clothes to come, and he came (this was when Henry disappeared, quietly) and Dan-boy grabbed hold of Sidney, who grabbed him round the neck and nearly strangled him so that they both went under for a bit, and Matt managed to catch the pole with the hook but he pulled so hard on it that it came out of the attendant's hand and fell into the water, and the other attendant leaned over to fish it out, but Matt's foot happened to tip the pole just as he had got his fingers round it so that he overblanced and fell in, and the water in the Baths became pale green and bubbling, with waves lapping up and down along the edges, because of all that was going on in it.

Eventually people and poles and water got sorted out, and Matt and Sidney were hauled to the side by Dan-boy and the attendant from the wire cages, who stood squeezing the turn-ups of his trousers while the other attendant gave the boys a lecture and propped his long pole back in its place again, and Sidney and Matt, very damp and humble, said thank you very much and no they wouldn't do it again, and they collected their clothes and dressed in double-quick time, so that the water was still running out of their hair and down the necks of their shirts when they stepped out into the street.

Henry was waiting for them, as arranged, in the shelter beside the bus stop. His hair was dry and his face triumphant. They didn't need to ask him anything, but he shook his pocket and they heard the sweet jangle of the keys inside it and knew he'd done his part of the operation successfully. So they padded back to Dove Square, not talking and keeping to alleys and back lanes, and finally through the alley between the Post Office and the newspaper shop.

Eddie was waiting, bored and sulky. He said he had nothing to report. The girls, he said, were still over at St. George Without. They'd been there for hours. Matt decided that it had been such a major victory that they could take the risk of celebrating it inside the railings after tea, when a full report would be given and future plans discussed. He announced this and went off in search of food. Drowning is hungry work.

An hour and a half later he stepped through the railings and wormed his way up the tunnel. He knew the others were there already and he had come late on purpose because something told him that this was an occasion, and it would be suitable for him to be the last to arrive. Henry was in the committee room, looking like a one-man committee. "They're waiting for you in the porch," he said. The committee room looked different. It had been swept and dusted and the windows were clear of spiders' webs. There was a strong smell of carbolic soap, the Reverend Robinson Crusoe had been polished and straightened and under his nose on the mantelpiece sat a jam pot primly stuffed with flowers. One of the bushes halfway up the tunnel was top-heavy with flowers like these.

"What's been going on?" Matt asked.

"Plenty, by the look of it — the touch of a woman's hand and all that. According to Eddie the girls have been at it all afternoon and they're no end pleased with themselves, so for any sake remember to tell them you noticed."

Matt promised he would, though he thought this sounded more like Gwen than Madge. Perhaps cleaning was infectious and Madge had caught it. He didn't think he liked the idea. But Madge looked the same as usual when he went into the porch except that she'd stuck a flower into her hair, like a gipsy, as if to make herself different from Gwen whose expression reminded him of his mother's after spring cleaning. Everyone looked rather unnaturally spruce and he noticed that the pale heads of the Flint twins were smarmed flat and darkened with water and that they'd put on their jackets.

He gave them the full story of the recovery of the keys, though he realized they must have had it already from Henry and Sidney. Nobody interrupted, but it wasn't more news they were expecting from him, it was something different. There was a triumph to be celebrated and he was to show them how to do it. He would know, since he was the leader, and their silence showed him that they were willing to be told.

Nobody said anything as he took the key out of its hiding place in the wall and unlocked the doors from the porch into the church and swung them open. They went in, not crowding and curious like the first time, but in a kind of rough procession of people who have earned a right to be there, with Matt at their head. He noticed that Gwen and Madge had been active here too. There were puddles of fading blue suds on the floor and a decided whiff of Brasso. When he came to the picture in the floor of St. George, Matt halted. Soap and water had been more effective than spittle and the colors in the mosaic were fresh and clear; the plates of the knight's armor, his plume lifted in the wind, the scales along the dragon's back, the rolling eye of the charger, the little landscape, all gleamed as if spring had newly broken out.

"You've cleaned it up well," he said.

Gwen smirked and said, "Madge helped."

" 'Try Holy-Suds and watch Satan run,' " Madge intoned in her telly voice. " 'Your church can be as clean as mine.' " It was hopeless to pay Madge a compliment. She hadn't changed.

They gathered round the picture in an expectant ring. If something doesn't happen soon, Matt said to himself, trying to dodge the glances in his direction, this is going to be terrible. It is very important that the right thing should happen. We're on the edge of something. I didn't ask to be out in front but I am. Somebody has to be out in front, and it's his business to know the right thing to do. That's what they're waiting for. But what is the right thing? And then someone in the circle shoved and one of the Flint twins bumped up against him and Matt felt something hard that was hidden beneath his jacket and guessed joyfully what it was.

"You've brought your bugles?"

They nodded, beaming, and pulled them out, breathing on their shining surfaces and buffing them with their sleeves.

"All right," Matt decided gratefully, "that's what we'll do. And we'll do it properly this time, remember. Come on, Henry!"

Henry gave them the note and the beat and they sang: "Ye gates lift up your heads on high!"

It isn't often that things go absolutely right for you when you are that age. Sometimes while you're still a little kid they do, or you think they do because you can make anything the way you want it to be by imagining that it is, and probably when you're grown up and have skill and experience you can do something that you know is perfect. But in between these ages, except for a rare occasion with a bicycle on a summery hill, or an obedient skipping rope, or a ball coming into your hand like a bird, most things you try to do have a sickening way of not being quite right and you know they aren't and everything is spoiled and it isn't worth trying. But it wasn't like that now.

Every note in the first verse was firm and true, no hesitation, no off-beat stuff from Sidney, they were all singing, and the sound of their voices with the bugles twining through them like ropes was so astonishing that when they had finished they looked at each other with a kind of triumphant alarm. But the second verse, as soon as they began it, was different. They weren't voices making music any longer, they were the instruments on which music was being made, just as the Flints' bugles were, and what was happening was and could only be perfect. The five Hallelujahs and the three Amens that followed were a solemn and amazed thanksgiving.

No one said anything when the last echo of a re-echo had breathed back at them. Even then no one said anything. Matt led the way out and locked the doors and put the key into its place and they went back to the committee room and squatted down, still silent and feeling a little dizzy. And Matt realized with faint irritation that the ball was at his toe again. There they are, he thought, like puppies that bring it back and back, and look at you happily because they are sure you will know the best thing to do with it next. He was getting tired of it. He thought it should be someone else's turn. But they were still waiting for him.

"Show us the keys then, Henry," he said, and Henry

took the bunch out of his pocket and they were passed around and gloated over.

"Gosh, Henry, I don't know how you had the nerve!"

"Just lifting them out of his pocket!"

"And it was you who paid for them to go in, too!"

"Gosh, Henry!"

"Sidney was pretty terrific too," Matt said, because Henry looked as if a halo and a string of medals were going to sprout out of him at any moment. "You ought to have seen him fooling away, up on the high board, and the way he fell in and pretended to drown!"

"Genuine pink-tickled whoopee," Sidney said modestly.

Eddie, when the bunch of keys came his way, passed it on quickly without saying anything. Matt got the danger signal, he should have seen it earlier. Eddie had been too quiet all along.

"Look what your clever Uncle Henry brought!" one of the junior Flints declared, dangling the keys for the Dragon's inspection. The cat dabbed a paw at them daintily, and set them swinging. Through the laughter Matt heard Eddie's dry snort of scorn.

"Pinching's easy," Eddie said, not looking at anyone. "Anybody can pinch."

There was a moment of complete emptiness, like a balloon that takes a long time to burst, and then Henry fired back, "And you should know."

Eddie smiled. "I do. That's what I'm telling you. Pinching's easy."

Gwen gulped and looked as if she was ready to explode. "You are horrid, Eddie," she scolded, "everything was so lovely, and now you're spoiling it all."

"I'm not spoiling anything. I was just wondering what Henry figured to do with the keys he'd pinched."

Henry turned dark red and mumbled that this was different, and Eddie agreed that of course it was; he'd pinched two batteries and a packet of Smarties out of Woollies and Henry had pinched the keys of St. George Without.

"I had a reason," Henry said.

"So'd I. My torch was flat and I hadn't any money left for sweets."

One of the Flints giggled and Matt said, "Shut up, you." He was angry with Eddie for mucking things up

and with the rest of them because now they were looking in his direction again.

"What Eddie wants to know is what are we going to
do with the keys. Anyway, what do you all think we
ought to do with them?" he asked crossly. "Come on,
make up your minds. That is if you've got any."

"Use them, of course," someone said grandly.

"What for?"

"For the Battle of St. George."

They nodded. It sounded good.

Eddie said, "And if the Police come nosing around
and find the keys on any of you—what do you suppose
happens then?"

"We explain."

Eddie said, "I'm not stopping you, but you can count
me out on any explaining."

"We only took the keys," Henry said slowly, as if he
was working out a sum, "so that Dan-boy and his pals
couldn't pinch the lead."

"Anyway, they weren't Dan-boy's keys. He pinched
them from Miss Harrison," Gwen said, putting another piece of the argument in place.

Madge threw a snake of hair angrily over her shoulder
and added, "And Eddie's only saying all this out of spite
because he couldn't go with the others to rescue Miss
Harrison's keys."

"That's right," they agreed, nodding.

"So they're Miss Harrison's keys," Eddie said, smiling
thinly to show it was a private joke, "so we give them
back to Miss Harrison where they belong."

There was a long unhappy silence. Eddie's vengeance

on them was bitter. "Well, come on, is that what we do?" Matt demanded. "It's for you lot to decide."

Rebellion stirred. "We can't just give them back."

"We wouldn't half look daft."

"She's going to think it a bit odd," someone suggested unhappily, "supposing she hasn't noticed they've gone. She'll think we pinched them from her."

"I see what Eddie means about the Police," Henry said.

"They wouldn't have you in the cathedral choir, old son," someone commented, "not if you'd been had up for pinching."

"Oh shut up," said poor Henry. Five minutes ago his had been a famous exploit. "I'd like to have seen any of you doing it."

"Eddie only wants to be nasty, anyway."

They snapped at each other like young animals. Only Eddie, smiling quietly to himself, and Matt, unhappy and angry, sat mute. Eddie hadn't half scored.

"I suppose we'll have to," Gwen said. No one contradicted her.

"Come on then," Matt said, "let's get it over with."

"Just hand them in?" they objected.

"What'll she say?"

"We can knock and leave them on the mat."

They got up, shoving bad-temperedly for the window. Matt had a thought. "Wait. Not that way." From the bunch of keys he took the second largest, the one Miss Harrison had told them was the key of the door from the committee room to the path outside. They stood round him while he fitted the key in the lock. The single use of this key would help a little to redeem the shameful but necessary future.

Matt turned the key and swung the door open. Someone was standing on the doorstep. "Strike me pink!" the figure exclaimed, backing.

"Corporal Frick," cried Matt gratefully. "Advance, Corporal, and be recognized!" And Shaky Frick with the little dogs advanced.

They were glad to see him. They were glad to have someone else to tell. And they told him everything from the beginning about the identity of Dan-boy, about Madge in the fish shop ("Smart piece of work there, young lady," Shaky said), about the stealing of the keys by Dan-boy ("Bare-faced and dastardly"), about the pursuit through the streets, the fun and games in the Baths, what Sidney had done and Matt and Henry, and how the keys had been recovered.

"Magnificent! A Major Victory!" Shaky declared. "And a classic example of timing and co-ordination and the intelligent deployment of personnel, if I may say so." They basked in his approval. No one mentioned Eddie's bombshell.

"And now I take it," Shaky went on, "you are completing the exercise by proceeding with the return of the misappropriated articles to their rightful owner, are you not?"

"Yes!" they agreed. "Of course!" Just like that. Meek as lambs. Of course that was what they were doing. "Will you come with us, Mr. Frick?"

"Well, I don't know about that." He looked doubtful. "I haven't spoken to young Queenie for some years. I'm not much of a social type myself. She knows that."

"Please. Please come," they said. And he agreed to come.

They set off down the tunnel through the bushes, which had been widened considerably in the last few days with the amount of traffic along it. Shaky and the dogs came with them. Matt was about halfway down the line.

"Get a move on, can't you," he said to one of the Flint twins who was directly in front.

"I can't."

"Why not?"

"It's Henry."

"Give him a shove."

"He says he's stuck."

"Then tell him to get unstuck."

"He says the person in front of him is stuck too!"

There was agitation and much whispering ahead. At last a message came down the line. "We're all stuck. The gap in the railings has been wired across. We can't get through."

Dismay like a tightening thread ran down the line. Matt passed the news to Shaky who was behind him.

"Aha!" crowed Shaky, "so the enemy's talking back, is he?"

"You mean Dan-boy's done it?"

"Sure thing. He's discovered he's lost the keys and

can't get in and he's making sure you can't get in either."

"We are in," a plaintive voice remarked, "we want to get out."

"File—About Turn!" Shaky ordered. "We shall use our alternative route," and Matt remembered the opening at the back of the telephone boxes.

The use of this exit was made warily; at last they were all through and had lined up in front of Miss Harrison's door.

Matt knocked and she opened it.

"Well!" she declared, sticking hairpins in furiously, "and you too, Charlie."

Corporal Frick stood to attention and said, "Pleasant evening, Queenie," and looked at the wall above her.

"Are you all coming in?"

"No thank you, Miss Harrison. Go on, Matt."

Matt held up the keys. "We came to bring these back to you. They're yours."

She stared and for a scalding moment they were afraid she was going to cry. Then her nose twitched and she put out her hand and he dropped the keys into it.

"I don't understand," she said, and turned and looked back into the room and saw the empty hook. "I didn't know."

They appealed to Corporal Frick for help. "You explain."

"There's nothing you need to know, Queenie," Mr. Frick said, "except to keep these out of sight. You may take my word for it that everything else is hunky dory."

"If you say so, Charlie," she said, "and thank you all."

She smiled. She noticed the children's sodden shoes with grass tangled in them. She said, "You've got your feet very wet, haven't you?"

They agreed they had, loving her for asking no more questions, and because now she knew.

She had noticed the flower tucked into Madge's hair. "You can have it if you like," and Madge surprisingly yanked it out and handed it over with a good helping of torn red hair attached.

There was an awkward silence. "Well, chin-chin then," Charlie Frick said, and young Queenie Harrison said, "Chin-chin, Charlie," and he saluted and said, "Till Hell freezes, Queenie," and after this astonishing exchange she smiled and went in and closed the door.

"What do you suppose all that was in aid of?" Matt asked Henry afterwards. "Like a foreign language, all that chin-chinning. And Honkey what?"

Henry said he hadn't a clue, but they were obviously on the same wave length.

"You can say that again," Matt said, "and how."

"Receiving each other loud and clear," Henry agreed. "Over."

"There's my Mum, I'm supposed to have the kettle on for supper, she'll be ready for blast-off. Over and out," Matt concluded, making tracks for home.

8

"NEXT please," piped the dentist's receptionist, popping her too-cheerful head round the door of the waiting room. The assembly of ladies stared at Henry who stared at his Christmas number of *The Bee-Keepers' Journal* as if he couldn't bear to lift his eyes from it even for a moment. Inside his ripely swollen cheek his tongue moved with caution.

"Who is next, please? Mr. Whittle is ready for his next patient."

The ladies jerked their heads at Henry. "Your turn, is it? Come along then, please," she said.

"I have to wait for my aunt," he growled without looking at her.

"He has to wait for his aunt," chorused the ladies in case the receptionist was deaf.

"Well then—whose turn is it?"

One of the ladies claimed the privilege and was led off towards the surgery.

Henry turned a page and tried to hum a careless little tune.

He knew the ladies were watching him. He'd already been in the waiting room for an hour and ten minutes. It felt like a week. For the last half hour he hadn't seen

The Bee-Keepers' Journal. For two days his whole world had been centered on this raging wild animal of a tooth. In the small hours of this morning he had decided that no one could possibly feel any worse than he was feeling, and this rash fit of desperation had brought him this afternoon to Mr. Whittle's door. Any moment now he would have to go into the Surgery and deliver himself, open-mouthed.

He didn't suppose the receptionist believed his story about his aunt, you could tell by the look in her eye that she knew it was only a delaying action. In any case it had all been a horrible mistake, he shouldn't be here at all. After all, his tooth was very much better now, in fact when you came to think about it his tooth was hardly hurting at all, yes undoubtedly his tooth was cured, he would just get up and slip quietly off home. The tooth at this moment stabbed him savagely back into his chair to show how wrong he was. He got the message and miserably flicked another page, envying bees their toothlessness.

"Too bad, dearie, your aunt never turning up," one of the ladies said.

He muttered something about her possibly having missed the bus, and hated the lady for her kindness.

"Of course if she said wait then you have to wait. But when a thing has to be done then the sooner the better, that's what I say. And that's one tooth you'll not be sorry to say goodbye to, isn't it?"

"Trouble getting them and trouble losing them," sighed another lady, and treated him to a pearly plastic smile.

Henry cupped his cheek in his hand and hoped the dark influences that were radiating from him would knock a few of them for six.

"Not fair, keeping the boy hanging around," the first lady said. There was a ripple of warm sympathy all along the row of chairs. Henry remembered with furious longing the days when you were young enough to roll on the floor and yell and stick your tongue out and make rude noises when you felt the way he was feeling now.

It was unfair that his tooth had flared up this week when all his money had gone on the Baths and he'd had none left for Nuttycrunches. Not a single sweet since Monday morning. If school had been on maybe he wouldn't have noticed the ache so much. But with nothing to suck and the Trailer hanging around saying, "Poor Henry's poor sore tooth," and nothing much happening inside the railings or out of them there hadn't been anything to keep his mind off it. He couldn't complain about it to the others, because he knew what they'd say; Madge had a particularly clever way of saying it.

There had been no further move in the battle of St. George Without apart from Corporal Frick's report that the old padlock on the main gates had been snapped off and replaced by a new one. Probably this had been done on the night that the entrance to the tunnel was wired up. "Think of it!" Eddie said disgustedly. "Us inside playing church while Dan-boy gets on with things outside." Since then nothing had happened. Nothing at all. What were the enemy up to? "Stick your heels in, lads, this is the war of nerves," Shaky Frick advised. Spells of patrol duty had been long, idle and empty — except for Henry's tooth.

"I mean it would all have been over and done with by now if your auntie had turned up like she said," the sympathetic lady remarked, "but I can understand that she wants to be here, just in case. After all, you never know."

In an effort to separate himself from her and from any other well-wishers he blew a little soundless tune out of the side of his mouth, carefully keeping the draft away from the sore place. It was, he realized, the tune of 'St. George's Edinburgh.' He'd got it on the brain, they'd all got it on the brain. Gwen had ridden on the front seat in Mr. Lumba's bus yesterday and she reported that he'd been singing it, very deep and supported grandly by the sound of the bus's engine (he must have caught it from Sidney), and Matt said he'd heard his mother washing the dishes to it, she'd picked it up from him. It was impossible to avoid it or to switch onto anything else.

The door opened. "Next please," the receptionist said again. Henry sweated fiercely and didn't move. She was looking in his direction. The squad of ladies came to his rescue.

"It's his aunt — he's waiting for his aunt."

"She said he was to wait."

"He thinks she must have missed her bus."

"He can't go in till his aunt comes."

Another lady rose and went off.

"Too bad," the chorus consoled him. "It could all have been over by now."

He put down *The Bee-Keepers' Journal* knowing that, aunt or no aunt, ladies or no ladies, next time the receptionist came she would winkle him out of his chair mercilessly. He stared at the wallpaper and discovered that it had stripes and decided in his extreme wretchedness to play the counting game. He did it during long sermons in the Cathedral and he was an expert.

So he counted the stripes on the wallpaper on all four sides of the room, adding up the total and dividing it by the number of sprawling cabbages on the carpet. He counted the pictures and photographs on the mantelpiece and multiplied them by each other. He counted the ladies with brown shoes and the ladies with black shoes and subtracted them from each other, taking his time to decide what to do about the lady whose shoes were navy blue. He counted the magazines on the heap in the center of the table and worked out how much they would fetch if they were sold at sixpence each, and to make it last longer, at sevenpence halfpenny.

Finally, since there was nothing else in the room to count, he looked out of the window. Ten cars parked in the car park, two of them green, five black, three red. He worked out the ratio. Four people queueing outside the butcher, no, five and a half, since a woman with a child had joined the queue. T. H. BRODERICK AND SONS, CONTRACTORS AND DECORATORS, written on a notice in the yard directly opposite. Six R's and six O's tied for first place. And there were two men in painter's overalls coming out of the gate from the yard, carrying a ladder.

In wretched desperation he counted the rungs on the ladder. This wasn't easy because the men were moving and the ladder was a double one, one of those ladders that extend to twice its height when it is required. This meant that the front row of rungs got mixed up with the row behind. He made the total eighteen the first time, but had a feeling he'd got it wrong so he did it again, and this time the men had slowed down to negotiate their way past the butcher's queue and so he had a better opportunity of counting. It came out as twenty rungs, and he was satisfied that this was right. Twenty rungs on the ladder, and since it was a double one, twenty rungs on the other half, and that made —

The realization of what that really did make took all sensation from his tooth for the first time in thirty-six hours. His joyful gasp was misinterpreted by the lady sitting next to him, who murmured, "Playing you up, is it?" but he never heard her. He had turned his attention from the ladder to the men who were carrying it and recognized one of them as the man who had come to the door of the shop to speak to Dan-boy on the day they had trailed him to the Baths. So that was it! They'd got what they wanted and they were taking it where it was needed and —

"Next, please," said the receptionist.

"Me!" cried Henry, bounding to his feet. "It's my turn!"

The ladies stared at him. "But what about your auntie, dearie?"

He said, "Blow my auntie," and stalked ahead of the receptionist into the surgery.

Fifteen minutes later he contacted Matt who was down on his knees in his mother's kitchen, washing the floor for her and for sixpence. Matt looked glumly at Henry and sat back on his heels, squeezing the dirty suds out of the cloth as if he'd had a spite against them. If the gang were feeling flat, Matt was flattest of them all.

"What do you want anyhow?" he grumbled. "I can't come now because I've got to finish this floor before my Mum comes back." He pushed the cloth wetly round in lumpy circles.

Henry squatted down opposite and told him. Matt stopped pushing and they stared at each other.

"That was what it was!" Matt said. "We should have guessed. Of course they'd need one that length for the high stuff!"

"And now they've got it."

"What do you suppose they're going to do with it?"

"Leave it where it suits them."

"Where? Which way were they going?"

"Up this direction, but I came by the alley, they'd have to take the ladder the long way round, we might get there first."

Matt gave the kitchen floor the quickest wipe it had had in its life, slapped the cloth back in the bucket and collected his sixpence off the shelf. "Come on. We might still be in time."

Like flies on a wall whom no one notices, like dry leaves blowing about in the autumn or little dogs very busy doing nothing in particular, they drifted up one side of Dove Square and round the corner into the next, looking at nothing and seeing everything. As they turned the second corner Matt spotted the white flag of a painter's overalls rounding the corner ahead. He dropped the sixpence into the gutter and they took their time finding it. The men with the ladder had reached the big entrance gates to St. George Without. They had propped the ladder against the railings. Now they were lighting cigarettes and chatting. One of them took a key from his pocket and unlocked the padlock that hung on the chain fastening the gates. He drew the chain clear and swung the gates open.

"They can't just do it that way!" Henry protested.

They could. They lifted the ladder and carried it inside, then laid it down a short distance from the gates, among bushes, and came out again, taking their time. Then they refastened the gates and went off.

"In broad daylight!" Henry gasped. "What a nerve! And anyhow why doesn't somebody stop them or ask them what they're doing?"

"That was much the best way for them to do it," Matt said. "After all, if you saw two painters open a gate with a key and put a ladder through do you think you'd go and ask them what they were doing? Do you suppose those men digging a hole in the road further up are meant to be doing it? Nobody told you. Maybe they just feel that this is a good hole-digging afternoon. But now we know that things really are moving."

He spun his sixpence joyfully, then caught it, and

stared at Henry and said, "I say, Henry, your mouth's bleeding."

"Is it?"

"Running down your chin."

"Oh that!" said Henry carelessly. "I had a tooth out this afternoon, didn't I tell you?"

"You — *what?*"

"My tooth, the one that was hurting. It was when I was in Mr. Whittle's waiting room that I spotted the men with the ladder."

"You mean you just went and he took it out!" Matt said. "Does it hurt?"

Henry tried and found it didn't. "Nothing to it," he said, "came out like a ripe raspberry."

"Well!" Matt declared. "We'll buy wafers from Mr. Ricardo's on the way home."

Mr. Ricardo was alone behind the counter; business at this time was slack. "Your Mamma just gone," he told Matt, "just this moment. Just too bad."

Matt explained that he was there on business, and Mr. Ricardo opened the ice cream tub.

"Listen," he asked, between scoops, "what tune is it your Mamma sings half the day? She sings it, now I sing it. Wait — I sing it to you." He sang a couple of lines of St. George's tune.

"That's right," Matt said. "You've got it. It's called 'St. George's Edinburgh.' "

"Soon we all sing it," Mr. Ricardo complained, "a tune like that you can't leave it alone."

Henry said, "There's a grand part in the second verse

where the tenors and basses come in on their own. Can you do that part?"

Mr. Ricardo was interested. "Show," he said. "Go ahead. You show."

Henry showed. "But who of Glory is the King?"

Mr. Ricardo tried it and agreed that it was good. They did the verse together.

"But there's a finale I have not yet got," Mr. Ricardo said, "an Alleluia. I ask your Mamma to show me but she says she is too busy to sing and yet all the time she works she sings."

"I'll show you if you like."

Mr. Ricardo liked. The shop was still empty.

"Take your time, stand up straight," Mr. Ricardo directed, "fill the lungs with air and open wide the throat."

Henry stood straight and the air from his lungs made the five Hallelujahs and the three satisfying Amens. Mr. Ricardo sang with him and they did it again. "Tomorrow," he said, "I sing the finale for your Mamma."

He made up the ice cream wafers, thick as doorsteps and with gobbets hanging out on all sides like icebergs and handed them over. He waved away Matt's sixpence.

"For free," he said, "for St. George."

9

THAT night Matt dreamed that he was back in the country again and that they were cutting the trees on the river side of the upper field. And in his dream he heard the saws sing and bite, and the squeal of the raw green timber, and the creaking groan as the great giants toppled, and the sigh of the branches settling on the grass where every year their leaves had fallen.

Half waking he remembered that he was living in Dove Square in the city — and then was full awake, stung with fear. He hoisted himself up on one elbow and edged the curtain aside and saw the substantial shapes of the trees inside the railings, solid against a sky that had already a thin hint of dawn.

The moon presiding just above the treetops looked like a skull. Across roofs and chimneys a clock struck three. Clocks in the city and cockcrow in the country to announce that the night is over but it will still be a long time until the morning. The trees were safe. It had only been a dream.

But he was restless, itching with a sense of necessity that he couldn't put a name to. Maybe I'm hungry, that's what it is, he said to himself, I'll go to the kitchen and cut a doorstep off the loaf and lay inches of butter on it and bring it back to bed with me and when I've eaten it I'll be ready to go to sleep again. He got up, pushing the curtains wide apart. The street lamps were still shining, but already they had a defeated look. The windows were still muffled by blinds and curtains and there was no light yet from any of them. The houses looked like high cliffs.

He felt lonely and ached for the morning. It was too early even for birdsong. A kind of excitement spiced with fear made him forget about being hungry. There was no time to be hungry, something was waiting to be done, he wasn't sure what it was but he knew he had to do it. The rest of the world was snoring with the blankets round their ears. This was his affair. He pulled on some clothes.

The stairs creaked as he came down them and padded across the empty landings. He resisted a notion to hammer crazily on the closed doors as he went by. He eased the chain off the hall door and opened it and went through, pulling it behind him. The colder air outside made him gulp.

He thought he imagined a flicker of movement from the window of the basement. Then the basement door clicked, someone was standing outside it, was coming up the steps. He almost panicked and ran, and then he saw it was Eddie and he stood and waited for him.

Eddie asked no questions. He just said, "May as well go together." He was dressed and looked as if he hadn't been to bed at all.

Matt asked, "What about Henry?"

"Well, what about him?"

"Better collect him, don't you think?"

Eddie shrugged but didn't object. Matt gathered a handful of soil and made a soft ball of it and chucked it against Henry's window. Then another.

"Come on," Eddie said impatiently, "no good hanging around."

"One more. His tooth had him hopping last night; he'll be harder to wake."

He threw a third ball against the glass, *plonk*. This time a pale shape showed itself briefly inside Henry's room. They went to the gate and crouched, waiting for him. He came yawning and shivering with his hair in spikes. "What's up?"

"We're going across. Want to come?"

"Oh all right."

It was only when they were moving to cross the road that they discovered the Trailer shadowing Henry. Any other time they would have laughed, he looked comic in his striped pajamas and bedroom slippers.

"What did you go and bring him for?"

"I didn't. He came."

"Well, he'll have to go back, that's all."

"He can't. The door's shut."

"He should have brought a coat."

"Well, he hasn't."

The Trailer jumped up and down looking happy.

"Well, I suppose he'll have to come."

The Trailer beamed and did kangaroo leaps.

They moved round the Square and into the trees through Corporal Frick's entry at the back of the telephone boxes.

"We might as well go and have a look at the ladder. If it's still there we'll know they haven't come."

Protesting birds squawked as they disturbed them, passing under the low branches. They worked their way round to the inside of the main gates. "Quiet!" Matt grumbled. "A herd of elephants wouldn't make so much noise."

They reached the place where they knew the ladder ought to be. They couldn't find it, excitement tightened, then their groping hands closed on it, hard and angled, lying in the undergrowth.

"We were wrong then," Matt said. "They haven't come."

They felt cheated and remembered how cold they were. None of them spoke until Eddie, running his fingers along the end rungs of the ladder, cried, "Look! It's all clodded up with earth. They've been using it." He slapped the earth off his hands. "But it's dry. They haven't been here tonight."

"When?"

"Last night," Eddie said, "or the night before. I was so sure it was tonight."

Henry said, "So you were wrong. What are we supposed to do now? We can't get in again, the door's closed."

"We can go on and spend the rest of the night with the Reverend Robinson Crusoe."

"I suppose it's all we can do," Henry grumbled. "It was a pity you had to be so sure it was tonight."

The birds sniggered at them as they made their way towards the church. They reached the clearing and crossed it. The drenched grass seeped into their gym shoes and the air seemed solid with the dew.

"It's still up there," Eddie said, staring at the roof where the streetlights caught the dull surface of the lead. "They haven't taken it yet."

Suddenly Matt stiffened. "Quiet."

"What is it?"

"Can't you see? The light. The light inside. They are here."

At the top of the windows of the church, above the boarding, was a light so faint that it was hard to tell if it was real or imagined until it moved, traveling from one window to the next, flickering, disappearing and appearing again.

"Are you sure it's them?"

"Who else?"

"What would they want inside?"

"Come on. We'll take a look."

"All of us?" Eddie asked. They understood what he meant and looked at the Trailer who was tightly hooked onto Henry's jersey.

"He can't come. If there's any trouble he's too little."

"He'd only be a nuisance anyway."

They argued fiercely in whispers of white breath that hung round their mouths like the balloons in a comic. It was decided to leave the Trailer outside the window of the committee room.

"You stay here and wait for Henry. We're coming back. And keep quiet—see? *Quiet!*" They went through the window neatly, leaving the obedient hump of shadow that was the Trailer outside.

They worked their way to the porch. The door into the church was faintly edged with light and the key was already in the keyhole.

"How did they know where to find it?" Henry breathed.

Suddenly Matt snorted and laughed out loud and kicked the door open. "Of course they knew! Who do you think it is?"

It was the girls and Sidney and the Flints, whose startled faces in the upthrown light from the torches they were carrying set the three of them laughing with a nervous, angry sort of laughter.

"What do you think you are doing here?" Matt demanded.

Gwen moaned, "Oh Matt, you've spoiled our lovely surprise!"

"What surprise?"

"He doesn't know. I told you he hadn't remembered. None of them have," Madge jeered.

"Remember what?"

Gwen explained. Tomorrow was St. George's Day. So they had brought daffodils and branches of trees and they were decorating the church. It was to be a surprise for Matt and Henry and Eddie. They got up very early to do it. You had to do something special for St. George's Day, hadn't you? *Somebody* had to do *something*. After all —

Before they knew it they were in the middle of a first-class row. Gwen had been too self-righteous about it by half. Madge had enjoyed mocking. The Flints were cross because they had been pleased to be given something important to do at last. Matt and Henry and Eddie were wild with themselves because they hadn't remembered April the twenty-third, St. George's Day. Anyhow, Gwen was carrying on now like someone who pretends that they don't mind when you've gone and forgotten their birthday, and Matt snapped, "You hadn't any right to come, any of you. It was strictly against orders. Nobody was to come unless they were on patrol duty."

"What are you doing yourself then, I suppose you don't need to keep to the rules seeing you make them," Madge sneered. She was carrying daffodils in her hand, you could smell the sharp outdoor smell of them, the torchlight shone through them, turning them into lanterns. Against the pillars, at their base, branches had been laid so that they seemed to grow like trees, and their shadows multiplied them against the stone.

"It's like a blessed Sunday School Treat or a Circus or something," Matt fumed. "You might have had more sense. Where did you get the daffodils from, anyway?"

"Off the top of Cousin Maudie's telly," Madge said with satisfaction, "she won't half give off when she finds out!"

"Who's been pinching now?" Matt asked, and was sorry when he'd said it because he felt Eddie stiffen at his elbow. The row dwindled into silence. And into the silence crept this other sound.

Matt looked at Eddie and Henry. They too had heard it. It was coming closer, slowly and not very steadily, but that was only to be expected once you had realized what it was.

"Quick!" Matt snapped. "The lights! All off!" Every torch was extinguished. People became shapes without faces. Matt whispered, "Quiet — quiet," and led the way back into the porch.

The sound was closer now. Below the crack of the heavy entrance doors a thin trickle of light was spreading. The sound had come very close. It increased further and then died altogether. Matt, bending to the keyhole, saw the headlights of the lorry.

"They've come," he said.

No one moved or spoke. They heard the men get out of the lorry and close the doors cautiously. Two of them were detailed to go and fetch the ladder. A voice complained that they'd lost an hour already, it would be light before they were through, and someone else retorted, "The job's half done. The rest's easy."

"What does he mean? Half done?" Matt whispered, and Eddie's voice answered, "I can guess. They cut the stuff last night or the night before, that was when they were using the ladder. Now they just load it up and carry it away."

"They *can't!*" Gwen's voice appealed to the Wrath of God.

"They can. Just watch them." Eddie's voice, fiercely amused.

"If they find us here — ?" A scared voice, one of the junior Flints, perhaps.

"We've got legs. We can run." Matt's voice, furious in defeat.

Then Madge's voice. "It's a good thing Henry had the sense to leave the Trailer behind."

There was silence. At last Henry's voice. "We didn't. He came. He's here."

"Where?"

"Outside. We left him outside the window."

"You *what?*" Madge cried.

It was a good thing that the men were by this time wholly occupied in hauling the ladder and setting it in its place, and that the sound of heavy dragging and pushing from the roof obscured the sound of Madge's indignation. No one had heard Madge like this before. Madge could be glum or rude or sarcastic or sometimes very funny if she cared to be. She never cared very much, one way or another, about anything. And so this torrent of honest anger took them all by surprise.

"So you left him outside, did you — like a parcel or something? You wouldn't leave a puppy outside in case it would whine and you left that kid there in the dark because you knew he wouldn't. I'll tell you this, Henry Mickle, I'm sick of the way you treat that kid. I don't think you ever talk to him except to tell him to shut up or do something for you. It'll be your fault if anything happens to him now, you know that, don't you? And there's another thing. I don't even know what the kid's name is, he never gets called anything but the Trailer, that's the way people think of him, the thing that gets hauled around and says nothing. What is his beastly name, anyway?"

"Bill," Henry said, in a queer kind of voice.

"Well then, we're going into the committee room

right away so that we can get Bill in here with the rest of us," Madge ordered, and led the way.

She hoisted herself up into the square of the window.

"Bill!" she called gently. "It's me, Madge. Come on. We're waiting for you. Come on, quick and quiet."

There was no answer. Madge called again. "Is it too high? Will I come and give you a leg up?" Still there was no answer. She turned into the room again. "It's too dark. I can't see if he's there."

"Of course he's there," Henry said crossly, "that was where we left him."

Eddie pushed Madge aside and leaned far out through the window. Then he pulled himself in again. "Madge is right. He isn't there."

"He must be."

"He isn't."

"I told him to stay till we came," Henry explained, but nobody was listening.

"Where do you suppose he is?"

There was a pause before someone said, "They've got him, that's what it is."

"They can't!"

"Well, what else?" Nobody had anything else to suggest.

"What'll we do now?"

If Madge had surprised them, Eddie had a further surprise to offer. "We tell the Police," he said calmly, "that's what."

"The Police!"

"But Eddie — *you* said all along — "

"I know what I said. Pinching lead is one thing, and it was all right playing our little game trying to stop them, we hadn't a hope really but it didn't do us any harm. And it didn't matter very much if they did pinch the stuff because if anybody minds that much about it they'll fork out for a new lot. But this is different, the Trailer, I mean. We can't do this on our own."

They thought about it. Someone said, "How do we do it?"

"Ring the Station from the phone box. I'll go."

Nobody argued, but someone said, "They'll see you from the roof."

"They won't."

Someone else asked, "Have you got any money?" and Eddie said, "You blithering idiot, don't you know yet that you don't have to have any money to ring 999?" and he went through the window as nimbly as the cat could have done it before anybody could say anything else.

He was glad there hadn't been time to argue, because now he was out in the open he was very frightened. He slithered into the grass and lay there, dredging the darkness with his hands in the place where the Trailer ought to have been in case he'd fallen asleep, but there was nothing there but grass. The men were working on the high part of the roof, he could just see their outlines, sometimes against a whitening sky, sometimes like shadows against stone. He skirted the clearing cunningly and reached the welcome cover of the bushes. No one had spotted him. He breathed more freely. The journey to the telephone box would not take him long. He noticed

169

that the main gates were closed, the men had closed them again after the lorry had been driven inside. He imagined the Trailer bundled into the back of the lorry. He felt a little sick. He worked his way to the gap by the telephone box. His face stung where small branches whipped it.

He had forgotten that the light in the telephone box burned all night. He would have to step out into the light.

The telephone buzzed and was answered and he said, "Police." His heart hammered as he waited. He felt stifled, and hoped there would be enough air in here for him to say what he had to say. He heard a policeman speak. He gave him the story. Men who were stripping lead off the roof of St. George Without in Dove Square had kidnapped a little boy. The men were preparing to load the stuff on a lorry. Yes, he was sure, he had seen it. Yes, the little boy had been fooling around in the grounds of the church and the men had collected him there.

Something in the blackness beyond the lighted telephone box was moving. The entrance gates swung open slowly. He knew that he had been seen. A man was coming towards the box, was standing there looking at him. It was the man whom he had expected. He had recognized Eddie and was smiling. Eddie said, "Please come quickly. The lorry is ready, they'll be leaving soon. You could pick it up if you come at once." He put down the receiver.

It had to happen some time. In a queer way he was

glad it was happening. Better get out of here, more
chance outside than cooped up in here. He pushed the
sucking door open. Now that fear had climbed so high
things seemed to straighten out in his head. If I can hit

him just once, he thought. I've been dodging him for weeks, having bad dreams about him at night, pretending not to be scared when I'm with the other kids and someone goes past that's like him, letting on I was mad that Matt didn't let me join in the spree they had at the Baths. If I can hit him once before he grabs me; once for all he's done to me, making me afraid, giving me orders, twisting my arm and smiling, knowing I have to do what he says because I'm the boy who was caught pinching out of Woolworth's and he knows how he can get back at me if I'm awkward, making me different from the other kids though I don't want to be different, so that even if I'm willing to play the sort of games they play I'm still different. Next time I meet him I'll be more his size, I can take care of myself. But this time, if I can hit him, just once —

Dan-boy moved quickly, his arm came out to grab him, and Eddie, experiencing a single moment of absolute happiness, ducked and hit him hard under the chin so precisely that he wanted to laugh from sheer pleasure. But his native sense prompted him to run and he reached the gap in the railings, Shaky Frick's gap, and was through into the dark tangling jungle of the bushes. He heard Dan-boy swear and lurch after him. His knuckles stung sharply and sweetly. He tacked and dodged and kept on running.

Sometimes his pursuer was very close, snatching at him and catching hold of brambles, stumbling and then coming on again. Eddie had gained a little distance by the time he reached the clearing. As he crossed it he heard the engine of the lorry running, the loading had been quickly done. He went through the window, but the committee room was uninhabited, they must have gone back into the church. He heard Dan-boy's feet kick against the stone, he was coming through the window after him. He'll never do it, he'll stick. As he reached the porch he heard Dan-boy's feet thudding on the floor. He had done it, he was through.

They were waiting for him inside the church, an anxious congregation of shadows. They reached out for him, and he made it, gasping, and they slammed the doors behind him and threw their weight against them. The man's footsteps were pulled up suddenly. Outside someone called, "Come on — we're ready! What's the holdup?" The man answered, "With you in a minute!" They heard his fingers fumbling for the lock, now he had found it, had discovered that the key was still on the outside of the door. He was laughing.

"Well, that makes things simple," he said, "thanks for everything." The key turned and the footsteps retreated. They heard the lorry revving up. It was off. The sound of its engine diminished and was lost altogether.

Silence grew round them coldly. "The kid?" Madge asked at last.

Eddie was still panting. "I told the Police. They know."

"Are they coming here?"

"They'll go after the lorry if they've any sense. I said it was just leaving."

After another interval someone suggested, "Then who will come here?" and another voice said, "Perhaps those men will come back."

"No," Eddie said, "they've got what they came for, plus the Trailer."

"What do we do, then?"

"We wait."

"So they won after all."

"I hit him," Eddie said, "just once, but it made a lovely noise."

This news consoled them a little, but now that the immediate tension had slackened they realized that they were cold and that their heads were dizzy, as if they were floating about in the air a few feet above their owners. There was still the unhappy thought of the Trailer and the niggling fear that the men who had locked them up might come back once their loot was stored. And if somebody else came and found them there was going to be an uncomfortable amount of explaining to be got through and none of it would be easy.

They could be sure of release by Corporal Frick's morning patrol at nine ack emma but long before that all their beds would have been discovered empty. And worst of all on the morning of St. George's Day, April the twenty-third, the roof of St. George Without was lying naked to the sky. The Battle of St. George Without had been lost.

They squatted with their backs up against the pillars, hugging their knees and their dismal thoughts. No one talked. Light in the church grew steadily. The dawn birds were making an unnecessarily joyful racket. Noises from the city told them that morning was now well advanced. The first milk van jangled its way along Dove Square. Traffic noises were building up. But none of this made them feel hopeful or excited. Nobody particularly wanted to be rescued now. They envied the statues above their heads, who had no problems and of whom nothing was expected. Life had become much too difficult. There weren't any answers.

Matt, stretched in a yawn, saw the daffodils that Madge had pinched from Cousin Maudie's telly and resented their cheerfulness. "Fat lot of fools we are," he said, "locked up like this on St. George's Day. I'll bet St. George is having a good laugh."

Suddenly Gwen came to life with a missionary look in her eye. "We ought to do it," she said. There wasn't a glimmer of enthusiasm, they were flat as cold pancakes.

Gwen said, "We came here to do it." You could imagine Gwen burning at the stake. "Come on," she urged, "what's the good if you don't?"

They grumbled, "What's the good if we do?" imagining a stake to burn Gwen on.

"I thought boys had guts," Gwen goaded them.

Someone said they didn't sing with their guts, but they unwound their arms and legs and stretched to get the stiffness out of their bones, and blew on their chilled hands, and stood up in a ragged, reluctant choir. The Flints, who had brought their bugles for what was to have been a triumphant occasion, now produced them. "Come on, Henry," Gwen directed.

Henry gave her a black look and said, "Oh all right. Are you ready?"

As they drew breath they heard the footsteps. It was impossible to tell how many footsteps there were but it sounded as they drew closer like a threat, like an army. Fear rekindled. So the men had come back after all.

The footsteps halted, a key had been turned in the outer doors of the church, now the army was advancing across the porch.

Unexpectedly Henry said, "Come on. One — two!" Well, why not? People sang when they were waiting for the lions to be let loose, people sang when the *Titanic* was sinking. We'll sing.

They began to sing and were singing as the key of the doors that separated them from the porch was turned, and the doors were pushed back and the daylight spilled in on them.

> *Ye gates lift up your heads, ye doors,*
> *Doors that do last for aye,*
> *Be lifted up that so the King*
> *Of Glory enter may!*

It wasn't the King of Glory for whom the doors opened, but an assembly of people almost as surprising. They identified them as their voices gained volume and confidence.

Miss Harrison, holding a bunch of keys. Corporal Frick, this time without his dogs. An elderly gentleman in a clerical collar beside him. Mr. Lumba and Mr. Ricardo, Madge's weird Cousin Maudie with her hair in curlers. Mrs. McGinley wearing an apron. Two policemen. Henry's aunt. Eddie's almost unknown Mum. The Trailer, carried on the shoulder of one of the policemen. Ma Flint with a glint of battle in both eyes at once. Gwen's big sister without any make-up.

It was easier by this time to go on singing than to stop and begin explanations. The newcomers had lined up across the open doors. Some had begun to sing. Mr. Ricardo and Mr. Lumba picked up their cue and came in with their lines strongly and clearly—"But who of glory is the King?" — and Henry threw the answer back at them straight as an arrow — "The Mighty Lord is this!" They finished the verse together.

The bugles made a timorous entry but gained authority and sustained the second verse. This was real singing now. " 'But who is He that is the King?' " demanded Mr. Lumba and Mr. Ricardo, richly and sternly. " 'The King of Glory who is this?' " echoed the children. And the reply came magnificently from them all: " 'The Lord of hosts and none but He, the King of Glory is! The Lord of hosts and none but He, the King of Glory is!' "

Five Hallelujahs and three Amens were hardly enough. Mr. Lumba had his shoulders back to it. Mr. Ricardo nursed the tenor notes to an impossible sweetness. St. George was celebrated.

When the last Amen shivered away Corporal Frick turned to the old gentleman and led him forward. "These are the children I told you of, my Lord Bishop," he said. The Trailer wriggled off the policeman's shoulder and headed full tilt for Madge.

≈ 10 ≈

"FOOD before explanations," pronounced my Lord Bishop, "we shall talk better on full stomachs." Gwen was speculating on the interesting probability of a fall of manna when Mr. Ricardo came forward with a different suggestion. "Bacon and eggs at the house of Ricardo. I should be most honored."

"How extremely kind. But — for this multitude?" The Bishop seemed doubtful.

"Mrs. McGinley and I, together we work the miracle," Mr. Ricardo assured him, and Matt's mother nodded at Mr. Ricardo and smiled and they all trooped across to Ricardo's and the miracle went into operation.

They talked while they ate and between mouthfuls of bacon and egg and toast and gulps of hot strong tea all the varied parts of the story came together. The Trailer's personal adventure was the most surprising; no one need have worried about him after all. But no one could go on calling him the Trailer any longer, they would have to get used to him as Bill, for he had become unhitched from brother Henry at last. After ten minutes in the dark outside the window he decided that he'd had enough of his semi-detached existence and since he was cold and sleepy he had had the wit to move to the one place where, at half-past three in the morning, he knew he could expect to find warmth and shelter — the Open-All-Night Launderette. The place was empty when he reached it, and in a chair beside the row of idle washing machines the Trailer — I beg his pardon, Bill — went purposefully to sleep until Eddie's Mum, arriving early to clean, discovered him and took him back to Dove Square and woke up Miss Mickle his aunt, who found that Henry's side of the bed was empty too. She, emerging onto the landing, met Matt's Mother, who was on early duty at the Restaurant that morning, and told her the story and she turned back to tell Matt and found that he was missing as well. Then Eddie's Mum began to get the general drift of things and went to check up on Eddie and found he wasn't there either, and so the babble of voices mounted and Mr. Lumba came out to see if there was anything he could do to help and behold Sidney's bed had no Sidney in it, and Miss Harrison from the bottom landing wondered what the noise was about and came to find out. They were joined by Cousin Maudie who couldn't lay her hands on Madge and Ma Flint who reported that her tribe had all taken themselves off during the night.

Meanwhile the Police, having had Eddie's phone call, had sent a police car hurtling after the lorry (it just succeeded in dodging them at the north corner of Dove Square and they were still chasing it) and the Sergeant at the Station rang up the Bishop to inform him of the vandalism at St. George Without because he didn't know whom he should inform and he was a man who believed in going straight to the top.

The Bishop when he heard the news remembered

that his secretary had mentioned something about an unknown Charles Frick who had been sending mysterious dispatches about St. George Without (she had filed them in a special file she kept which she labeled "Dotty," but the Bishop didn't know about that) and his Lordship asked the Police car that came to fetch him from the Palace to call at Mr. Frick's lodging on the way to the church, and Shaky Frick (who was not at all surprised, he'd been expecting the Bishop for weeks) told his Lordship that the keys of the church were to be obtained from his friend Miss Harrison, who lived in Dove Square.

So when the Bishop (with Corporal Frick as escort) arrived at Dove Square to ask if they might borrow the keys to make a thorough inspection of the damage to the church, they walked straight into a dismayed mob of fathers, mothers, aunts and sundry other relations, discussing up and down the landings and staircases, across fences and basement areas, what could have happened to their children who should all have been eating cornflakes at this time in the morning. Corporal Frick's suggestion that they might be over at St. George's was pooh-poohed at first, but Bill (insofar as they could get any sense out of him, he was so sleepy) seemed to agree with Corporal Frick, so the whole assembly including the Police had headed for the church, with Mrs. McGinley calling in at the Restaurant to let Mr. Ricardo know she might be late for work. And Mr. Ricardo had downed dishes and come along as well.

The pleasant unreality of bacon and eggs and hot tea blessed by a Bishop in Mr. Ricardo's at eight o'clock in the morning made the children very conversational, so that they almost forgot who had won the Battle of St. George Without, and told their part of the story with relish, what they had done and what even cleverer things they had intended to do, and how everyone had helped to do them. All the details were spread out and enjoyed, like marmalade on buttered toast, relations forgot to scold, and even Cousin Maudie declared she was delighted that her daffodils had gone to honor St. George. Mr. Ricardo and Mrs. McGinley, talking gaily to each other and to everyone, went up and down the tables with teapots and toast racks and more dishes of marmalade and replenished plates of butter. Bill, the ex-Trailer, was half asleep in Madge's loving lap. Ma Flint was looking unrecognizably benign. And Matt, sitting dazed and stuffed, had just enough sense left in his head to realize that it wasn't only the breakfast that was a miracle on this morning of St. George's Day.

"Now," announced the Bishop, setting his empty cup finally in its saucer, "my young friends and I have matters to discuss. Alone. And if I may borrow the keys from you again, Miss Harrison, I propose that we hold our discussion in the committee room over at the church." So Miss Harrison gave the bunch of keys to the Bishop and he headed the procession, a much smaller procession this time, back to St. George Without, entering it decorously through doors unlocked by his Lordship.

They found a packing case on which to enthrone him and the rest of them sat about on the floor. The Bishop looked like an elderly eagle hunched on a small rock.

His beaked face studied them but it was impossible to tell how much he saw through the thick lenses of his glasses. The Dragon appeared from nowhere and sat down in their midst, staring boldly at the Bishop.

"Now that I've had the whole story from you," his Lordship began, "I think I am right in concluding that you have had what might be called —" he chose the word carefully —"a whale of a time."

This was a new line in bishops. Their breakfasts cooled uneasily in their stomachs. It wasn't over yet. They hoped that the Reverend Robinson Crusoe on the wall was on their side.

"Correct me if I'm wrong," the Bishop continued, "but as far as I can see you have told lies and trespassed and deceived your parents and used violence and taken the law into your own hands and stolen what was not yours and run unwise and unnecessary risks. Isn't that so?"

Their silence unwillingly agreed with him. The Dragon rose and walked up and down, rubbing himself enjoyably against the dark columns of the Bishop's trousers, purring like a traitor.

"Why did you do it? Can you tell me why? There must have been a reason."

There was a long silence. But they knew that when this old gentleman asked a question he intended to have an answer.

"For St. George," someone hazarded at last.

"Who was St. George? Do you know?"

"He was — he was a famous hero, who did famous

deeds and fought battles and rode on a charger."
Henry's information came stickily.

"He was a most great guy," Sidney said.

"And rescued maidens in distress," added Gwen.

"Like Jack the Giant Killer," the Bishop suggested and no one contradicted him, "or somebody out of a Western." He scratched the cat cleverly under its chin. "Any other reason?"

Matt said, "They hadn't any right to take the lead."

His Lordship nodded. "Neither they had. Any other reason?"

"Mr. Frick told us what would happen if the lead was stripped off and the roof fell in."

"What did he say?"

"That demolition squads would come with bulldozers and knock down what was left of the walls and the church would disappear, and they'd cut the trees, and the ground would be used for something else."

The cat rolled over and permitted the Bishop to rub his stomach. "Mr. Frick was right in what he told you," the Bishop said. "This is what will happen."

They bristled. "But the church! St. George Without! People wouldn't allow it!"

"Why?"

"They — they like the church to be there."

"For a museum, or a lucky charm, or something? No one has been near the church for many years, you know that. It didn't make any difference to anybody that it was there."

"What about us?" Gwen challenged. "It made a difference to us. There are fifteen of us altogether."

He eyed her over the top of his glasses. "If you are trying to do an Abraham act over me, young lady, then I'm gratified that you know your Bible, but let me remind you I am not Jehovah."

Gwen turned raspberry pink.

"Let me put it this way," the Bishop continued, "if the Diocesan Council and the Trustees of St. George Without decided that it was possible to spend thousands of pounds putting the church in order, who would come to it and pay for its upkeep?"

It wasn't any good saying "us."

"People need churches," Madge glowered.

"People who feel they need a church don't let one rot when it's on their doorstep. And if there isn't one and they need it they go out and shout for one to be built," the Bishop said.

"There aren't enough of us," Henry said.

"Not at the moment," the Bishop agreed, "but things are changing, just as this part of the city is. Before ten years are up all the houses in Dove Square will have been pulled down to become shops and offices, and you will be living in flats or in estates on the city border. Did you know that?"

Their faces showed that they hadn't known. "We don't want things to be changed," someone objected. "It won't be the same."

"Neither will you. In ten years you will be grown men and women out in the world bringing home wage packets, and if you shout loud enough you will get churches built near your new homes and you can go to them and take your families."

"We'll shout," they said.

"Be sure you know what you're shouting for. Not the old things, it'll be something different, something valuable to your generation. And the churches will be different too, not like St. George Without. They'll be made of glass and concrete and whatever other material the new generation of architects considers functionally suitable for the worship of the Almighty."

"What will happen to St. George's?"

"The Diocesan Council may decide to sell the land for some other purpose, and the money will help to pay for building the new churches."

Henry objected. "But the ground is holy. It's been blessed."

"Yes," the Bishop agreed, "but there will be dotted lines on the architects' plans for the new churches, and you can be sure the Almighty will make these areas holy too, when the time comes."

"Everything's holy," Gwen said chummily, "that's it, isn't it?"

"Everything can be holy," the Bishop agreed, "it depends how we use it. And thank you for what you have done. Even in the things you shouldn't have done you showed a kind of — faithfulness. I like that. I'm glad it made a difference to you. I may say — " here he took off his glasses and wiped them and his unshielded eyes blazed at them suddenly — "that it has also made a difference to me."

For that single moment they loved him ferociously. "Come on," he said, "time we were going. We must lock up first. Let's be grand and go out through the main doors."

In the porch he halted. "What's that small door for? Do you know?"

"That's where the bell is."

"The bell? Is there a bell?"

They nodded.

"Still there, is it?"

"Miss Harrison said it was left because bells are hard to shift."

There was a silence into which the idea grew like a mushroom.

"That's the key for the door," someone volunteered, "that little one."

He selected it from the bunch. They watched while he fitted it in the lock and turned it and opened the door. The rope, draped in cobwebs, was hooked against the wall. The Bishop unhooked it and balanced it across his palm.

"You pull it," someone said.

"Shut up, you nit. What do you suppose he thinks you do with it — suck it?"

"I'll bet the rope's rotten."

The Bishop tested it. "No, it's strong enough."

There was a pause. "I always wanted to ring a bell," the Bishop said contemplatively.

"Every St. George's Day they rang it," Gwen said, breathlessly casual. "That's the proper day. Miss Harrison told us."

"Ah!" said the Bishop. "She did, did she?" and took off his coat.